**She leaned into his shoulder, placing her hand over his galloping heart. "I just wanted to pretend like it was all over for a second."**

Tempting to let her...to let himself. But not yet. It was hard to think about what would come after, when there was so much in the here and now that didn't make sense. But eventually it'd be over.

She rubbed her hand against his heart. "This is special. It feels special."

He closed his hand over hers. *Special.* It seemed like a weak word...but whatever this was, this hard, twisting thing in his chest that felt like some mix of terror and elation, it was special, and it was important. "It is, Hilly. It is." He pulled her hand off his chest. "But—"

"But we're in the middle of danger. That's the only thing holding you back, isn't it?"

"No. Not the only thing." He knew the next words would hurt her, but he also knew she needed to hear them. Maybe coming from him it wouldn't be so bad.

"Hilly, you don't know who you are."

# WYOMING COWBOY MARINE

---

## NICOLE HELM

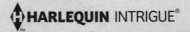

HARLEQUIN INTRIGUE®

For the Harlequin Intrigue readers who supported a brand-new
Harlequin Intrigue writer. Thank you.

ISBN-13: 978-1-335-64079-6

Wyoming Cowboy Marine

Copyright © 2019 by Nicole Helm

Recycling programs
for this product may
not exist in your area.

Printed in U.S.A.

**Nicole Helm** grew up with her nose in a book and the dream of one day becoming a writer. Luckily, after a few failed career choices, she gets to follow that dream—writing down-to-earth contemporary romance and romantic suspense. From farmers to cowboys, Midwest to *the* West, Nicole writes stories about people finding themselves and finding love in the process. She lives in Missouri with her husband and two sons and dreams of someday owning a barn.

## Books by Nicole Helm

## Harlequin Intrigue

### *Carsons & Delaneys: Battle Tested*

*Wyoming Cowboy Marine*

### *Carsons & Delaneys*

*Wyoming Cowboy Justice*
*Wyoming Cowboy Protection*
*Wyoming Christmas Ransom*

*Stone Cold Texas Ranger*
*Stone Cold Undercover Agent*
*Stone Cold Christmas Ranger*

## Harlequin Superromance

### *A Farmers' Market Story*

*All I Have*
*All I Am*
*All I Want*

*Falling for the New Guy*
*Too Friendly to Date*
*Too Close to Resist*

# CAST OF CHARACTERS

*Cam Delaney*—A former marine who is now starting his own security business. Drawn into the case of a missing person, Cam gets way more than he bargained for.

*Hilly Adams*—A young woman who's lived off the grid for as long as she can remember. When her father disappears, she seeks the help of police. When they can't help, Cam Delaney steps in.

*Laurel Delaney*—A detective with the Bent County Sheriff's Department, and Cam's sister. She asks Cam to help Hilly find her father.

*James Adams*—Hilly's missing father.

*The Protectors*—The anti-government group Cam and Hilly infiltrate in order to find James.

*Zach Simmons*—A member of the anti-government group. His secret identity unlocks Hilly's past.

# Chapter One

Cam Delaney did not care for being ordered around. It had been one thing in the military. A way of life, one with a clear hierarchy. He could take an order from a superior officer, no problem.

In Bent, Wyoming, the only hierarchy he paid any attention to was the fact that he was a Delaney, and no one told him what to do. There were no superior officers, because he was it.

His little sister hadn't gotten the memo.

"I have a situation," Laurel said with no greeting as Cam stepped out of his truck. He'd parked in the lot of the Bent County Sheriff's Department thinking he'd meet Laurel inside, but here she was waiting for him.

"I told you not to agree to marry a Carson, but—"

"Not that," Laurel returned, not even cracking a smile or offering some sibling teasing back. Which could only mean she was in full-on cop mode. "I've got a woman in here trying to file a missing persons' report for a man who doesn't exist."

Cam slid his hands into his pockets, trying to find some patience with his bullheaded sister. "What's that got to do with me?"

Laurel sighed as if Cam was a special kind of stupid, which didn't make him any happier about being summoned. "There's not much I can do to help her in a professional capacity. But you—"

"*I* run a security business. For profit. We're not private investigators, and we don't work for the sheriff's department." It wasn't a *we* as of yet, but Cam had plans. Big plans.

"There's something here." She glanced at the squat building that acted as Bent County's sheriff's department. "I can't put my finger on it, and I don't have time to figure it out. But you do."

"Laurel—"

"What big bad security jobs do you have? You're just getting started. If my town gossip is correct the only job you've been hired for is watching Frank Gainville's cows."

"He had a serious potential cattle-rustling situation happening," Cam replied loftily.

"Wasn't it some teenagers trying to hide their pot?"

Small towns. Why had he decided to move back to one?

Unfortunately the answer to that question was something he wanted to dwell on even less than he wanted to do Laurel's bidding. "Still solved, Deputy. Which is more than I can say for you and whatever this is."

Laurel nodded toward the building, a sign for him to follow her. "Woman came in wanting to file a missing persons' report. Subject has been gone for a week. Not uncommon he goes off for a few days, but a week has never happened."

"Sounds routine enough."

"Would be. She didn't have his social security number or any pictures, so we ran him to find a social or a photo from the driver's license."

"And you can't find anyone by that name?"

Laurel opened the door and waved him inside. "It's a common enough name. But we tried every spelling and none of our hits are him, according to the woman. The man she's trying to find doesn't exist in any records we have."

"I still don't see what that has to do with me."

"She seems lost. She needs help, Cam, and

I can't do it. It's outside my job description, and I have a wedding to plan that could very well implode the whole town. I'm telling you, there's something about this thing that makes me itch."

He knew that kind of itch. He'd been a Marine for fifteen years. Most people got gut feelings, but military and law enforcement people tended to hone this sense, and to listen to it more closely than civilians.

*Except you, when it matters most.*

"Just talk to her," Laurel urged. "See if you don't get the same feeling I do."

It took Cam a few seconds to bring his mind from his biggest failure back to the present and his little sister asking for his help.

He would never be able to make up for the ways he'd failed in the past. His conscience ate at him, a black worm of rot that had led him not to re-up with the Marines. That had led him to come home, and try to find some way to help the people of Bent, the people of his blood and bones and history.

If he could help, he should. He would. It would be something to do anyway, and Laurel was right. His fledgling security business wasn't exactly swimming in customers. Bent was isolated, but he hoped his military background might be lure enough to get some outsider customers. There was a big mine over in Fremont. Some ritzy folk with ranches here and there. He had plans. Big plans.

"Cam?"

He blinked at Laurel and the note of concern in her voice, and the softening features of her face. The last thing he wanted from Laurel, or anyone in his family, was sympathy. Because sympathy was only one step away from pity.

"Who's the man who doesn't exist? How is he related to the woman reporting his disappearance?"

Laurel gave him a raised-eyebrow look as she held open another door and gestured him inside. "Her father."

DAD WOULDN'T BE HAPPY. That thought sat uncomfortably in Hilly's gut as she sat in the small police station.

But he'd been gone a week. He never disappeared for a week. Three days, tops, that was the rule. So, she'd waited three days. She hadn't really worried until day five. For the past two days she'd searched for him herself.

He'd never been gone this long, and he hadn't left her with the tools to survive without him. She didn't have contact with the outside world. Only he did.

Why hadn't she questioned that more? Why hadn't she insisted on him giving her more understanding of what to do if he never came back?

He had to come back.

She swallowed and looked around the station waiting room. It was mostly empty. Occasionally the front desk phone would ring and the man on duty would answer. Mutter a few things, then hang up.

The people in this place kept telling her there was no record of her father. Had seemed generally baffled by their inability to find any information on him.

It was a mistake, was all. Maybe when Dad had moved them off the grid fifteen years ago he'd somehow wiped out all record of himself. It was possible. It was… It had to be true. After all, there was no record of *her* anywhere.

But Dad had grown up in the outside world. He'd only taken them off the grid because he'd wanted her to be safe. The outside world wasn't safe, and you couldn't trust anyone.

Which was why she had to leave this police station. She couldn't be here. This was a mistake. If something happened to Dad, it was up to her to figure out what. It was up to her to save him.

What had possessed her to think outsiders should handle her business?

Panic. Plain and simple. She didn't know how to survive without her father, and she couldn't *find* him.

She would have to figure this all out on her own, because you didn't trust the outside world. It was only ever out to get you, and that was why there was no record of Dad anywhere. He'd kept her safe, and she'd risked her and his safety all because of panic and fear.

She had to get out of here. Fix this. Disappear back to her life because her life made sense.

She got to her feet a little abruptly, and the man behind the counter raised an eyebrow, but she couldn't worry about that.

She had to get home. Away from the outside world and all its strangers' secrets and lies. She'd go home and double-check to make sure Dad hadn't returned in the time she'd wasted making the trek here and back.

If not, she'd mount a real search, and she wouldn't stop until she'd found him. And if she never found him…

It wasn't possible. She couldn't think like that.

She walked for the door, coming up short when the woman from earlier came through it, holding it open for another person behind her. A man. A large man with hazel eyes that seemed to move over her and file every little detail away.

She didn't like that. Anyone with that kind of interest in a stranger wasn't to be trusted. They both weren't to be trusted, even though the woman had been kind enough.

You couldn't trust kindness from the outside world, Dad had always said. You couldn't trust, period.

So why had he left?

"Were you going somewhere?" the woman asked gently.

Hilly didn't remember what she'd said her name was. Hilly had been out of her mind with panic when the police officer had introduced herself, and their inability to find a record of Dad had been the reality check she'd needed to get her back home, to take care of this herself.

They were probably lying about Dad not showing up in their computers. Computers. That was how the government kept you under their thumb. How they used you against your will.

"I just realized how silly I was being," Hilly said, doing her best to sound calm. Maybe a little chagrined. "He's a grown man who can take care of himself." *And I'm a grown woman who can take care of myself.* Dad hadn't given her any skills to deal with outsiders or the outside world, but she knew how to survive.

They always survived.

"We'd like to help, if we can," the woman said kindly.

*A lie.* Besides, the man behind her looked anything but calm. He looked... She couldn't even come up with a word for it. It was almost like a void. He didn't give anything away. "I don't need help," she returned, forcing her gaze to return to the woman instead of the man.

"Ms. Adams, you came to us for a reason. Because you're worried about your father. Now, I know we can't find a record of him, but that doesn't mean I don't want to help."

"It's very kind of you," Hilly said politely. "But I think I overreacted. I can handle it from here."

She scooted in between them and out the door, doing her best not to run. They would find running suspicious. She wanted them to forget she existed, not suspect anything. None of this was their business, and she'd been stupid and dead wrong to think it would be.

She hurried through another doorway and

then out the front of the police station. *Idiot*. The word looped in her brain like a chorus. If Dad found out, he'd be furious. She had to get home and make sure he hadn't returned.

It was a four-mile hike, but it would give her the time to plan and get ahold of herself. She walked around the building of the station to the back and the bushes where she'd stashed her backpack. She'd been afraid they'd want to search it, and she didn't want anyone finding her revolver.

She opened the pack and checked its contents. Everything was how it should be. She pulled the gun out and stuck it into the back of her jeans. It wasn't comfortable to hike like that, but she wanted to be prepared. She'd stash it away again once she was on safe ground.

Any place where buildings and cars could be seen was not safe ground. Other people weren't safe. Ever.

She adjusted her pack, the gun in her waistband, and then was about to set out toward the trees and mountains when the man rounded the corner of the building, opposite the way she'd come.

He stopped when he saw her. "Ma'am, can I talk to you for a second?"

His eyes dropped to her arm as she slowly

moved it to her back, where she rested her hand on the butt of her weapon. He seemed to know, somehow, that was exactly what she was doing as he raised his gaze very slowly and carefully to hers.

"Are you in some kind of trouble?" he asked. There wasn't a kindness or gentleness to his voice like with the policewoman's, but his tone wasn't nearly as hard as his body was.

"A strange man is accosting me in a parking lot."

His mouth quirked, and Hilly's stomach swooped. She felt breathless for a second in the joy of that smile.

Dangerous, dangerous man.

"Leave me alone, stranger," she said with some force.

He didn't say anything to that and, as she walked away, keeping him in her sights to make sure he didn't follow, his gaze stayed on her the whole time. Until she disappeared over a hill.

She had a bad feeling those hazel eyes would haunt her for a while.

# Chapter Two

It crossed a line.

Or one hundred.

Cam had never been big on crossing lines. He believed in rules, in law and order, and doing what was right. But one thing his time in the military had taught him was that sometimes following rules or orders *wasn't* right.

The woman was scared of something. He'd watched from behind the corner as she'd pulled the bag from the bushes, taken the revolver out and shoved it in her waistband.

She was spooked. *Lost.* Clearly the woman needed help and she was afraid to ask for it. He couldn't just let her disappear into the woods never to be seen or heard from again.

Where the hell was she going without a car? With that backpack and gun? Something didn't add up, and maybe it wasn't precisely right to give her a ten-minute head start and then follow her trail, but it wasn't precisely wrong either.

It further added to his suspicions and that *itch* Laurel had mentioned when the woman's trail wasn't easy to follow. Like she was purposefully covering her tracks.

But with the mix of soggy ground from snow melt and snow itself as he moved to the higher elevations, he'd been able to follow the imprints of impact, making an educated guess what was human-made.

When he'd gone roughly a mile, he considered heading back. He wasn't prepared for a hike. He was wearing tennis shoes that were now soaked through, and he only had his cell phone and keys, no pocketknife or water.

But no matter how many times he kept telling himself to turn around, to forget this woman and the *itch* she caused, his feet kept propelling him forward. His eyes kept watching for signs of disturbed earth or snow so he could follow her trail.

At three miles, he was 75 percent sure he'd lost the trail or was following someone else's. How could this woman be walking this long and this far? It might explain the backpack, but it sure didn't explain anything else.

So, he walked on, following the trail another full mile, cursing himself with every step. But the trail became clearer, as though she'd given up on hiding it. As if she didn't believe anyone would follow her this far.

As he continued on, he reached a clearing and peered through the edge of tree line where her path went. He frowned at the little cabin in the middle of the clearing. It looked rough-hewn and cobbled together out of disparate pieces. Something out of time, really. He could see some old miner or mountain man living in that shack back in the day, but not a young woman in the 21st century.

More, he was about 90 percent sure this was public land, and he was 100 percent sure there was something very wrong here. A man who didn't exist and a young woman living in this hideaway cabin on public land.

Cam could only assume the young woman was an innocent bystander. She had reported the man without an identity missing, and unless she was suffering from some sort of mental issue, he imagined she was unaware of whatever was very wrong here.

He surveyed the clearing, the shack, trying to get a sense of things. Not just a layout, but a mental picture. It felt good to put his brain to work this way, even without any plausible answers. Since he'd left the Marines last year, he'd had a floating sense of uselessness, even with solving the case of Frank Gainville's cows. Something about *this* felt like being of use.

Some of that disappeared when the woman stepped out of the shack with a flourish, a dog at her side and a gun in her hand. Not the revolver from before. She'd retrieved a rifle. She pointed it directly at him and the dog immediately began growling.

Cam held very still. "That's a slightly bigger gun than the last one," he offered, eyeing the animal with some trepidation. It was a big dog, at least part German shepherd. It growled low in its throat, clearly poised to strike at her command or at her letting go of the leash.

She didn't say anything, and the dog snarling on the chain wasn't exactly comforting, but there was something familiar in all this. A dangerous situation. Wanting to help. Having to rely on his wits.

He'd *missed* this.

He breathed in the icy spring air and tried not to smile. He had a feeling she wouldn't appreciate the smiling stranger who'd followed her home.

"I didn't get your name back there."

She didn't say anything. She kept the gun trained on him and the dog's leash loose around her wrist. To an extent she matched the cabin: out of time. Her reddish-gold hair was pulled back in a braid and the wind whipped loose strands around her face. She had a sharp nose dusted with freckles, and a glare that would probably scare lesser men. She wore battered jeans and a long, heavy coat that also whipped in the wind, and boots that had seen better days.

Add a Stetson and replace the jeans with a skirt and she could have easily fit in the old Wild West without anyone looking twice.

"Move into the clearing," she ordered, her voice low and calm with none of the nervousness she'd displayed at the police station.

He did as he was told, stepping forward. He held his arms up. "I'm unarmed and I'm not here to hurt you."

"You followed me four miles. What *are* you here to do?"

"Figure out the truth."

"The truth is none of your business."

"I only want to help." As true as it was, he could admit he'd made a misstep here. Just because he sincerely wanted to help didn't mean a woman should believe a strange man wanted to help her. "I'm not here to hurt you."

"Except you don't know me. So you don't

know what might hurt me. That's far enough," she said when he took another step toward her.

"Fair point," he said, pausing in his steps. "But I want to help you find your father."

She narrowed her eyes at him. "Why?"

"Put down the gun and we can talk about that."

If anything, she firmed her hold on the rifle. "How about you talk or leave, all while I hold this gun? Do not take another step or I will shoot you," she said after he'd taken another one closer to her and her dog.

"You're not going to shoot me," he said calmly, keeping his arms up as he carefully edged toward her. If he was calm, she'd be calm, and he didn't think she had enough anger or fear in her right now to shoot him.

But the sound of a gun going off and the sharp sting in his arm happened at just about the same time. He looked down at his arm, the slight tear in his jacket and shirt and the blood now trickling out of a slice in his skin.

"Okay, you *are* going to shoot me," he muttered at the mostly superficial wound.

"The next one will be worse," she warned.

He no longer doubted her.

HILLY KEPT ALL her panic below the surface. You had to be calm when facing the outside world, and Dad had never believed she could be. That was why she had to stay hidden away. That was why he handled anything that meant leaving the property.

Shooting the man hadn't been calm, not by a long shot. Especially since she'd only meant to scare him...not actually hit him.

At least she *appeared* calm from the outside.

On the inside? Panic city. Actually shooting the man advancing on her *had* been panic, even if she hadn't exactly *meant* to.

Could he put her in jail for that? Surely not. She'd warned him, and he'd been coming at her. It was self-defense, intent or not. She hoped.

Where was Dad? Why had he left her alone like this? She didn't know how to deal with it. With this stranger. Who was now staring at his arm where she'd shot her glancing blow.

It could have gone worse. She could have hit him somewhere vital, done significantly more damage. But he'd been *advancing* on her and home and...

"You should go get that looked at," she said. Even though her heart and pulse beat hard in her neck, she *sounded* calm, and like the kind of woman who shot people every day.

But would he go home and tell everyone

about the girl in the shack he thought might shoot people every day?

Oh, this was a *mess*.

"You've shot me now—you can at least give me your name."

She shook her head, not trusting her voice.

"What are you so afraid of?"

Everything. The fact she wanted to trust the kindness in his voice even though Dad had told her to never trust kindness. The fact she'd somehow involved someone in this. She was very afraid of everything that existed beyond this clearing.

She'd braved it today because she'd been out of her mind with worry about Dad, but never again would she think she was strong enough to handle the world out there.

*Except, if something happened to Dad you'll have to.*

She eyed the man and his bleeding arm. He said he'd wanted to help find Dad, but why should she trust him? An outsider who wasn't even a police officer in any way she could tell.

But maybe that was good. Dad said you didn't trust police, but men were motivated by one thing and one thing alone. Money. If he wasn't police and she offered him money…

*Except the whole you-shot-him thing.*

Free kept growling low in her throat. Hilly had to think. She had to get this man out of here.

"Go away, mister."

"You expect me to hike the four miles back with blood dripping down my arm?"

She wasn't sure why, but she got the impression this man could handle it well enough. Still, guilt pricked at her conscience. Though it shouldn't. She owed him nothing. He wasn't just an outsider, he was an aggressor.

He'd stalked her. He hadn't listened to her warnings. He deserved that wound on his arm, and yet that little seed of guilt sprouted and tried to surface.

"I'll get you a bandage, and then you can be on your way." She crouched down and scratched Free behind the ears, whispering her command. "Free. Guard." The dog growled in agreement, her eyes never leaving the man with the bloody arm.

Hilly hurried back into the cabin. They had an extensive first-aid kit, but it was kept hidden away behind all the daily necessities. Dad insisted anything of value or that hinted at having more reserves than for a few days be kept out of plain sight.

She could pay the man outside. She could pay him to find Dad. No, she didn't trust him, but it was an option. Enough money could keep a man under your thumb, Dad said, and there was money. Hidden in drawers and sewn into mattresses. She didn't even know how much was hidden in this cabin, but she could use it to find her father.

Who wouldn't approve of getting help from the outside world.

It was stupid. Impossible. She could not trust this man who'd *followed her*. Whom she'd shot.

But she didn't have anyone except Free, and as handy as dogs could be, they could not communicate, investigate or lend a hand with obtaining supplies from the outside world.

Dad had left her alone. She had to survive that, which meant she had to make her own decisions. Not ones Dad would make.

She gave herself a moment to close her eyes and take a deep breath. Take stock of the situation. Dad was missing. She was on her own. A strange man had followed her home under the guise of help.

Dad would scare him off. Hilly had no doubt about that.

She thought about the woman officer she'd spoken to at the police station. The woman had been in charge. Of herself, of her job. She hadn't looked to anyone for help. She'd made the decisions and she'd told other people what to do.

Hilly had been in *awe* of her. She wasn't allowed to call any shots, and Dad didn't listen to her about anything. Not that he was mean about it. It was just that Dad was in charge. Dad made the choices.

And Dad had left her alone. Which meant *she* was in charge, and when she found him—no matter how—Dad would just have to accept that. Because he hadn't left her with the adequate tools to deal with this. Hopefully now he would.

*If he's alive.*

She shoved that thought out of her brain as she got to her feet. She held the bandage in her hand, and though it went against everything she'd ever been taught, she left the rest of the first-aid kit out.

It felt thrillingly wrong. She nearly smiled as she stepped out the front door. Except the sight in front of her stopped her short in shock.

Free was on her back, wriggling joyfully as the large man rubbed her belly.

"You little traitor," she muttered.

The man smiled up at her, and it felt like something unleashed low in her stomach, fluttering upward and into her throat. She didn't care for that sensation at all.

She still had her gun, though, so him turning her dog into a pathetic little affection fiend was only taking away *one* of her weapons. Not all of them.

She aimed the gun at him again as she held out the bandage. "Here. Now be on your way."

He eyed the gun as he slowly got to his feet. Free whined. This close Hilly was uncomfortably reminded of just how *large* he was. Tall and broad and someone who could definitely outmuscle her if he wanted to.

But she had a gun. A gun. She tightened her grip on it.

"Are you going to shoot me if I reach for that?" He motioned to the bandage.

"Not if you reach for that and that alone."

His mouth curved, some foreign thing in his eyes. Something like laughter, but sharper. Her cheeks heated. But he carefully reached for the bandage and plucked it from her outstretched fingers.

He shrugged off his coat. Then, in a mesmerizing move, he tore the sleeve from where it was ripped from the bullet. Two tugs and the sleeve was completely off, just a few threads hanging down over his biceps.

His arm was…an arm. Why was it fascinating? Dark hair dusted his forearm, but his biceps looked smooth, except the slight slash of the cut and the smudge of blood around it.

"I could help you, you know," he said conversationally as he wound the bandage around his cut.

She wrenched her gaze from his arm and the easy way he dressed it as if he tended wounds every day. "I—I'd have to trust you," she said, hating herself for the stutter. "I don't."

He nodded thoughtfully, then those hazel eyes pinned her where she stood. "What would you need? To earn your trust, what would I have to do?"

*Nothing. Nothing at all.* Which was just stupidity and she would not be stupid. That was what Dad would expect her to be. Too innocent and weak-willed to find him, to survive.

Well. She'd just have to find him and prove to him she could make choices, too. Even if it meant trusting an outsider.

## Chapter Three

She looked confused for a few seconds, then something like determination chased over her face. Too bad Cam didn't know what she was determined to decide.

He finished wrapping the cut and picked his coat back up, pulling it on again. He ignored the shudder of cold that worked through him. "You're worried about your father."

"I am," she said, chin lifting. "He goes away sometimes, but never this long."

"And you don't know where he goes?"

She paused. Not the kind of pause that preceded a lie either. That lost look in her eyes from the sheriff's department stole through her once more, though she quickly hardened against it.

She was definitely young, but not *that* young. Early twenties, if he had to guess. She was strong enough to fire off a warning shot, kind enough to get him a bandage and smart enough not to give him her name.

No number of strange situations he'd found himself in as a Marine prepared him for this puzzle.

"I didn't actually mean to shoot you," she said, eyeing him. He noted it wasn't an apology.

"I know."

"How do you know?"

"If you'd meant to shoot me, I'd have a lot bigger hole in my arm. Clipping this close without doing much damage? That's pretty much luck of the try-to-get-close-enough-to-scare shooting variety."

She studied the bandage he'd tied off, then him. "And you know a lot about shooting?"

"Enough."

"You want me to trust you for no reason, and then you're evasive?" she said with such utter contempt he had to believe she'd been hurt before. There was a reason she and her father were tucked away here, and judging from the weapon she'd used on him and the one she'd carried with her, cash flow wasn't the problem, or the only one.

Unless the guns were obtained illegally, which was always possible. Too many questions. Not enough answers. Mostly, she was right not to trust him and find his evasion lacking.

If he wanted to help her—and he couldn't explain to her or, even worse, to himself, why he wanted to help her—he'd need to offer up some truths. Besides, offering truths to her was better than finding the answer to that question inside himself.

"My name is Cameron Delaney, though I go by Cam," he began, trying to think what would be important for a scared young woman to know. "I grew up in Bent, Wyoming. If you've ever been there you've probably heard of the Delaneys. My sister was the deputy you spoke with. I was in the Marines for almost fifteen years, but I decided to come home last year and open a security firm. Hence the knowledge of guns and shooting them. Is there anything else you'd like to know?"

"Why?"

"Well, there aren't a lot of security options in—"

"No, why did you leave the Marines?"

He had practiced responses to that question. Responses he'd given his family and friends. The rote answers weren't coming right this second. He had to search for them.

"It was time."

"Why?"

"It's grueling, and I wasn't…" *Fit*. He'd known he wasn't fit for duty anymore. Not with Aaron's suicide hanging over him. Not with that utter failure to notice, to help. He hadn't been able to get past that.

"You weren't what?" the woman demanded.

He owed her nothing. He could turn around and go home. He had all the choices in the world. But if he could help her… If he could help people, surely at some point it would make up for what he hadn't helped.

"A man in my unit committed suicide." His voice sounded rough and strained, and he wasn't sure what he expected the woman's response to be, but she only blinked. "I had a hard time coping after that."

"They kick you out?"

"No, I was granted an honorable discharge." Honor. What a laugh.

"If I let you help me, what's in it for you?"

"Having helped," he replied with all the sincerity he had.

"You don't know me. What would helping matter?"

He shouldn't be baffled or irritated by her

pressing the issue, demanding some kind of proof he was a decent human being. She shouldn't believe he was. She shouldn't trust him. "Haven't you ever helped someone simply because you could?"

"No."

"It feels good. There's a pride to having helped and having done the right thing."

"So. You're going to help me find my father. Then what?"

"Then I go about my life and you go about yours." Assuming the father was missing under some kind of favorable circumstances. There was always the chance he was dead, or that he'd disappeared on purpose. Cam didn't need to tell her that, though. Either she knew or she didn't need the worry.

"Just because you want to help someone. Because it feels good."

"You don't believe me."

She didn't respond, but she looked at his arm. Even though he'd put his coat on, he had a feeling she was thinking about the fact she'd shot him. "How would you help?"

"I'd need some information about—"

She shook her head and patted her leg, the dog jumping to stand next to her. "No."

"No… No?"

"No information."

Something was so completely wrong here. People didn't live off the grid for no reason, and he might have been able to chalk it up to some innocuous thing like environmentalism, but the woman's evasion coupled with her utter lack of trust in a stranger meant all things pointed to *shady*.

"How can I help you find your father without information?"

She shrugged and started walking to the shack door. "I guess you can't."

"I have to know what he looks like. His name. Where he may have gone. I can't wander around not knowing anything about the man I'm trying to find. If you don't give that information to anyone, no one can help you."

She stopped at that, her back still to him. She didn't turn as she spoke. "I don't think he goes by his name out there," she said quietly.

"Out where?"

She sighed irritably and turned, making a broad arm gesture around them. "Beyond here."

An uncomfortable chill shivered down his spine. Something was seriously wrong here. "What's beyond here?"

"The outside world. That's where he goes, and I don't think he uses his name out there. Maybe that's why the police couldn't find records of him. He must use a different name." Her eyebrows drew together, and she looked confused and definitely worried.

Whatever was off here, Cam had the sneaking suspicion this woman wasn't part of it. She was in the dark about this "outside world." Who talked about things like that? "And you don't go into the outside world?"

Her brown eyes widened a little, but she kept the rest of her expression carefully blank. "I did today."

"But that was rare. You don't have transportation."

"We have a horse."

"But *you* don't. Still, that helps. A middle-aged man on a horse. What are the names he answers to?"

She let out a shaky breath. "He wouldn't want me to give out his name. He wouldn't want me to have gone to the police."

"But you did." Cam couldn't make sense of her fear, because it didn't look like the kind of fear he'd experienced or seen. She had such a calmness, such a handle on it, and yet he could sense that what vibrated inside of her *was* fear. "How long have you lived here?"

Her eyes snapped to his, sharp and on the offensive. "My life and his are none of your business. Poking into us isn't help, *Cameron*."

"No one calls me that."

"Guess what? I do." She squared her shoulders, somehow looking imperious and regal even though he was taller and broader and just so much larger than her small, narrow frame. "I'll pay you to—"

"I don't ne—"

"I'll pay you to help me, mostly because I need transportation. But the money I'm giving you means I don't have to answer any questions I don't want to, and it means you go away when I say. I'm using you as a tool to help *me* find my father. That's it."

He eyed the shanty of a cabin. "You don't have to pay me."

"Those are my terms. Stay put."

CAMERON MADE HER ACHE. It wasn't an ache she fully understood. It twined around her much like when she was sick and wished someone would take care of her. There was this yearning for something she couldn't fully grasp because she'd never seen it in action, only read it in the fiction books Dad used to bring her from his trips outside.

Dad. Missing. Dad, who would hate that she was taking help from anyone. But she needed help. It was *Dad's* fault she needed help.

She strode into the shack, Free at her heels,

though the dog looked longingly back at the big man in their yard. Longing. Hilly didn't understand it, or what exactly she was longing for, but it was there regardless.

She tried to put it out of her mind as she forced herself over the threshold of Dad's room. He didn't like her in here unsupervised. She had her own tiny closet of a room after all, and he never invaded *her* privacy, did he? She was only allowed in here to monitor his security setup, or fix it if anything was buggy. To come in and snoop through his things? Unheard of.

But she had to force all those old rules out of her mind and habits as long as Dad was missing. She was an adult, and she could handle any disapproval she got from Dad as long as she brought him home.

*Do you need to?*

That internal question stopped her in her tracks. It echoed inside of her, and something desperate clawed at her chest. What if she just got to live her life her way?

No. No, she didn't know how to do that. She went for Dad's desk and pulled out one of his ledgers. He worked on them sometimes in the kitchen, so she knew he kept track of supplies bought, money in from the odd jobs here and there and money out on said supplies. And that he would stash cash in between the pages of said records.

She flipped through the first one, pulled out a few hundreds. She had no idea what the going rate was for a fake detective helper, but she'd offer Cameron a hundred up front. If he laughed, well, she could up it.

She glanced at the monitors set up across Dad's desk. Cameras that kept watch on the entirety of the woods that surrounded the cabin. They were always taping.

She'd already gone through the footage of the day Dad left, and she'd watched what he'd taken and which direction he'd gone, but it didn't tell her anything. Everything had been usual, ordinary.

Maybe she should show it to Cameron. Maybe he'd—

Her brain stuttered to a stop as two men appeared on the east side of the cabin. Men with weapons.

The front door opened, quiet and with just the tiniest creak she only noticed because she was holding her breath. She looked around the room quickly, but Dad had all of his weapons hidden away.

"Free, guard," she whispered, but the dog laid happily by the bedroom door, tail swishing calmly. Today of all days her dog was completely failing at every command she usually followed unerringly.

But then *Cameron* stepped into the room. "Someone's out there."

He was warning her. She didn't know what to do with that so she glanced back at the screen where she saw the two men slowly inching their way toward the cabin.

"They see you?" she asked quietly.

"I don't think so. I heard them more than anything. I thought it could be your father, but two people seemed ominous."

She pointed to the screen. "Friends of yours?"

He frowned at the two men on the video, studying them closely. He shook his head. "I know most everyone in Bent, or I did. Those two don't look familiar. They're armed, though."

Again Hilly nodded sharply. In all their years here, in all Dad's excessive surveillance, they'd never had unwanted visitors that Hilly knew of. She knew he had his reasons for being careful, and she'd never questioned them...to his face.

"You don't know them?" Cam asked gently.

*I don't know anyone.* But she didn't say that out loud. She studied their faces, trying to find some detail that would give her an idea of what they were after. "Maybe my father sent them. To get me a message."

"I don't know that messengers would carry Glocks, or sneak around the woods outside your cabin."

"You did."

"I didn't sneak, per se."

She spared him a glance, but when he only smiled at her, she quickly turned her gaze back to the screen.

Free started to growl, low in her throat, as if she sensed or heard the approach. "Easy," Hilly murmured.

"What are you going to do?"

"We're going to wait. And watch." She glanced around the room. The cabin only had two windows. One here, facing the west, and one in the front facing the east. "Go close the curtains in the front for me," she ordered. "Lock the door."

"Already locked," he said, even now on his way out front to close the curtains. She watched the screen with growing alarm as the two men conferred about something, and then split up.

Cam returned and Hilly couldn't think about how much her world had changed in just a few hours. Being in her father's room, with a *man*, two other men sneaking around her cabin.

"You might want to get one of those firearms you're so free and easy with," Cam said grimly. "I don't think a locked door is going to keep those two out."

Hilly broke her gaze from the monitors. She quickly moved through the cabin, gathering the rifle and the revolver, before she returned to Dad's room and Cameron.

A strange man in her father's room. She couldn't fathom it even as it was happening. "I also have shotguns," she said.

He nodded. "Get them."

After a brief hesitation, she handed him the revolver and the rifle before she strode to her father's closet. She knew his shotguns were in a hidden compartment at the back of it, though she didn't think her father knew that she knew that.

But he wasn't here, and she was in danger. She turned to study Cam. Was she really going to trust this stranger?

When she heard a rattle at the door, she knew she didn't have a choice.

## Chapter Four

Cam studied the unfamiliar guns. He had experience with a wide variety of weapons, so he'd figure them out no problem, but it was still strange to hold another man's—or woman's—weapon.

"Shells?" he asked.

"Everything is loaded."

He raised an eyebrow at her as the rattling on the door became more pronounced. He had certainly walked into *something*, and completely unprepared at that. It wasn't a particularly good feeling, but he wouldn't let that show. He was a former Marine. He knew how to handle a few surprises.

"Who would be after you?" he asked, shoving the revolver in the waistband of his pants much as she had, and testing the weight of the unfamiliar rifle.

"No one," she said flatly.

He gestured to all the security monitors.

"People with this kind of security, loaded guns and refusal to give their names aren't usually innocent bystanders."

He watched her expression change as he spoke. A kind of confusion as if she'd never considered how over the top the cabin's protections were. But then those eyes trained on him, determined all over again. "But you're inside with me, instead of out there with them."

She didn't seem scared exactly, but she did seem concerned and puzzled. If she had a clue what her father's dealings were—whatever they were—she would have more fear than confusion. She also wouldn't have gone to the police and she certainly wouldn't be letting him be in here with her. Not when she was clearly capable of shooting someone.

"What could they want?"

"I don't know." She shook her head and scowled, reaching behind the monitors and turning them off. She grabbed a tarp-looking thing off the floor and threw it across the screens. "We'll hide for now."

"Hide?"

"Well, I'm not going to shoot them."

"You shot me."

"Accidentally," she said, striding into the closet again. She ordered the dog to come and it obeyed. Then she looked expectantly at him.

"What do we accomplish if we hide?"

"Maybe we hear something they say. Maybe they take something and we know what. Maybe—"

A cracking sound echoed through the cabin, as though the people outside had broken something on the door. Cam quickly grabbed his phone out of his pocket and brought up the voice-recording app. He placed the phone on the floor, under the desk.

It wouldn't pick up anything unless someone came into this room and talked, but it was worth a shot. He heard the slow creak of a door opening and slid into the closet with the woman and the dog.

She pulled the door closed. It was a small closet, but it was obvious a lot of the space was taken up by a false wall and the array of weapons the woman was now covering up with some kind of panel that fit perfectly into the opening.

Cam was having a harder and harder time believing she was some innocent bystander. Who lived in a shack with this kind of hidden weaponry, an array of surveillance, and people missing and breaking in? Because if she wasn't involved, surely she'd be more than mildly perplexed.

He couldn't hear anything outside the closet except random muffled noises, but he wasn't unused to waiting in still silence, unable to move or talk no matter the cramped, uncomfortable circumstances. He knew how to control his breathing and avoid panic. This was all part and parcel with what his adult life had been.

He was a former Marine. He could stand quiet in a closet for a little while.

There was the small and unusual factor of having to do it with a civilian woman he wasn't sure whether to trust or suspect, though.

He couldn't make her out in the dark space, but he could hear the soft inhale and exhale of her breath, could occasionally feel the faintest brush of her arm or leg or the dog's.

The closet smelled of the tangy hint of mothballs, and the dog clearly hadn't had a bath in a while, but cutting through those disparate smells was her. Wood smoke and leather.

Rough, outdoorsy smells, but her hair kept wisping across his cheek, soft as a feather.

He didn't care for the fissure of unease that spidered along his skin. Something was wrong. *She* was wrong. Everything about the situation told him she was not what she said she was.

And yet, he believed in her. Felt better served keeping her safe in here rather than engaging with the strange men who'd broken into her house. Regardless of what she wasn't telling him, what the truth was underneath all this confusion, he couldn't help but believe this woman was a victim of…something. That was what his gut told him.

Except she wouldn't even tell him her name. He'd accepted that when they'd been outside and he'd been trying to gain her trust, but her giving him a gun changed things. It meant he had some power—he'd be loath to use—and it signaled her trust was building. *You could at least tell me your name*, he thought.

But before he could ponder further, the low sound of murmuring voices infiltrated the closet. The woman moved into a crouch, and Cam realized she was doing something to keep the dog from growling or barking.

Cam held himself still, straining to make out what the voices were saying. He couldn't, but he had to hope that if he could hear a murmur in the closet, his phone was picking up actual voices.

Cam had no idea how long they stood there, quiet and trying to breathe carefully and silently. The voices disappeared, but the occasional creak or groan of the house kept them in place. They couldn't leave the closet until they were sure the men had gone, and every time he got close to suggesting they ease their way out, a new sound was heard.

He couldn't figure out the sounds he heard now. Almost like water pouring, the occasional snap that sounded like someone stepping on a twig. It was a shame they couldn't have brought her extensive security monitors in here with them.

Something acrid tinged the air, and it only took him a moment to recognize the odor. Cam swore and began to feel around for the doorknob.

"What are you doing?" she whispered.

"Smell that?"

"Smoke, but… Oh my God. You don't think—"

"Where there's smoke, there's fire," Cam said grimly, trying to find the knob in the dark. "We have to get out of here. Now."

CAMERON HELD HER back as he struggled to open the door. She was about to tell him to back off when the door swung out. Then all she saw were flames. Huge red flames licking up the walls of her father's bedroom.

Her mind went completely blank for a moment, and she just stood there staring at the horrible sight in front of her. The flames danced and moved and took over more and more space. The smell and smoke stung her eyes and nose, and her throat began to burn.

And still she stood in the closet, even as she realized the buzzing in her ears wasn't a side effect of shock, but the actual sound of fire eating through wood.

It took her a few seconds to realize Cameron had moved. As if nothing was on fire, as if this was completely normal. He walked right across the room to the small window and used the butt of the gun she'd handed him to break it.

He held his arm over his mouth and quickly and efficiently pushed as much glass off the edges as possible. Then he grabbed the linens off her dad's bed and threw them over the windowsill.

He looked back at her, and something about the way he just seemed to know what to do reengaged her brain.

"Grab the dog," he commanded.

Her eyes were stinging so badly she could barely see through the painful tears, but she crouched down and wrapped her arms around Free. It wouldn't be easy with Free's weight and size, but she whispered calmly into the animal's ear as she hefted her up and struggled toward the window.

Cameron's arm brushed hers as he reached around Free and helped to lift her high enough so they could give her a gentle toss out the window. She landed on all fours and immediately began barking incessantly.

"Now you," Cameron said, and his firm, calm tone steadied her. "Be careful. I cleared it as best I could and the sheets should keep you from getting any cuts but don't put undue pressure anywhere."

She nodded and leveraged herself out the window. It was awkward and painful, but she managed to tumble to the ground without any major injury. Free rushed over, licking her face and whimpering. Hilly got to her feet, petting the dog in the process. She looked at the house, completely engulfed in flame, and couldn't begin to wrap her head around what was happening.

But one thing she could wrap her head around was the fact Cameron hadn't climbed out after her. She rushed toward the broken window. "What are you doing?" she yelled as Cameron moved deeper into the room.

"I've got to get my phone."

"Are you stupid?"

"Keep an eye out. Whoever started the fire might still be around," he instructed, getting down on his hands and knees and disappearing into smoke and flames.

Free whined from her position away from the flames and the heat and Hilly knew she should move back and away. She could feel the rawness in her throat from too much smoke, and nausea was curling itself in her belly.

Cameron was in there, the biggest moron to ever live, but a moron who'd gotten her and her dog out of a burning building first.

She wasn't about to risk *her* neck for a phone, but she couldn't convince her body to move away from the window where smoke billowed out. What was he doing? What if he *died* in there? Some kind of idiot who thought he was impervious to fire.

But then he was climbing out the window, pulling her with him as he moved away from the flames and smoke. The area around the cabin was completely filled with smoke so it took a while to reach fresher air.

His cough sounded tight and terribly wheezy, but he held up the phone as if he'd won some prize. Free whined at his heels as they walked and walked until the air was more clear than smokey.

He held the phone out to her.

"Dial 911," he rasped.

She blinked at the phone he'd shoved into her hand. Dad had one, but she'd never been able to use it. *A real woman doesn't have any use for a phone or the outside world. Her home is her domain. Everything out there is a threat.*

Cam coughed some more, but Hilly could only stare helplessly at the screen. There was only one button on the contraption and it didn't seem to do anything.

"Cam, I…"

The quizzical look he gave her made her stomach churn almost as much as the nauseating smell of smoke. He was bent over and struggling to breathe, his hands on his knees, and she didn't know how to do what he asked.

He took the phone back and poked his fingers against the screen. It seemed to do what he wanted and he stood to his full height, holding the phone to his ear.

"Uncontained fire," he said in that military voice, commanding even with the hoarseness from smoke inhalation. "I don't have an address, but I can explain somewhat where we are." He gave pretty clear directions in that strained voice, not coughing until he'd hung up the phone.

"You don't know how to use a phone," he said.

"We don't…believe in phones." Which wasn't true exactly, but it seemed less embarrassing than saying she wasn't allowed to use them. She was a grown woman, and as much as she didn't understand that world out there, she'd seen enough in that police precinct to know women used phones and likely did whatever they wanted.

That was the danger in it, after all.

"I'm going to call Laurel." He coughed again, and it still sounded awful even if his breathing had eased somewhat. "We'll wait for the fire department." He surveyed the fire charring and melting her home of the past nearly twenty years into nothing. Provisions, money, equipment. Everything she'd ever owned, everything she'd ever known. Gone.

It was a large clearing, and the conditions weren't dry, the ground a muddy wet from the spring thaw, but Hilly knew enough to know a fire like this could get out of control anyway. Her home might not be all that went up.

She only realized she was shaking when Cam took her by the arm. His hand was big and gentle. Even though his grip was firm it was very careful.

The shaking intensified, like she'd been shoved into icy water. Her teeth were even chattering and suddenly she did feel cold. Cold and sick.

"Sit."

She looked up at him helplessly, but he nudged her leg until it buckled a little. She didn't fall exactly, because he was holding on to her arm. It was almost as if he had the strength to simply lower her to the ground like that.

"Sit. Breathe. It's okay to feel off. You're in shock."

"Shock," she repeated. Free whined and crawled into her lap, muddy and shaking a little herself. There was some kind of relief in that, and she leaned into Free's truly awful-smelling fur and did what Cam told her to do. She sat. She breathed. All the while he talked into his phone in low, raspy tones. She didn't even try to make out the words.

She should try to hear. She had to protect herself. Protect Dad.

But her house was on fire. Their life was on fire and Dad was missing and all that was left were the clothes on her back and Free.

She'd even left Dad's weapons in there. He'd be so mad. So mad.

"Hey." Cam was crouching at eye level, sympathy softening his features so much he almost didn't look dangerous. He almost didn't look like a stranger. For a blinding second she could almost believe he was a friend.

*Don't be stupid, Hilly.*

"It would help a lot if I knew your name."

She shook her head, and had to close her eyes against the flash of anger in his. But he didn't lash out. He didn't yell and he didn't hurt her. He rose. "Can you walk?"

She swallowed and dared to look up at him. He stood there, arms crossed over his chest, a serious, determined expression on his face. Whatever anger or irritation had been there was gone now.

"I can walk," she managed. She nudged Free off her lap and got to her feet. He wrapped his hand around her arm again when she swayed.

It was strange. Her arm tingled like there was something chemical in the contact, but her shirt was long-sleeved so they weren't touching skin to skin.

Skin to skin. How...odd.

Once she was steady, he let her go and began to make his way through the trees in a slow circle around the house that still blazed and smoked. "We'll see if we can see anything. A clue as to who did this. We might get some footprints. The fire department should be here soon, and once we've talked to them and know we won't be interrupted we'll listen to what I recorded."

"Do you really think your phone picked up any—"

He stopped on a dime near the front of the house, so quickly she almost ran into his back. He frowned at the now-familiar sight of burning building, and that was when Hilly saw it.

Spray-painted haphazardly in the muddy grass of the front yard was one word.

*Confess.*

She could practically *feel* Cam's suspicion sliding over her and weighing her down. But she had nothing to confess. She'd committed no crimes. She'd barely ever left this cabin or clearing since she'd moved here when she was a little girl. Whatever this was, it wasn't anything to do with her.

"I don't have anything to confess. I can't even think of one possible thing."

"You're not the only one who lives here, though."

"You think this is for my father?" But, of

course it had to be. She wanted to believe it was a mistake, but… Dad had disappeared. Someone wanted him to confess. "It has to be a mistake."

She hated the pitying expression on Cameron's face. He thought she was *stupid*. She wasn't. She knew it could only be about Dad. But it didn't mean it had to be *right* about Dad. And it didn't mean she had to…

"It's fine. Believe whatever you want. Don't tell me your name or his name. That's your choice. I can't help you the way I'd like, but it's your choice."

*Help you.*

No one ever wanted to help her. She existed to help Dad, not the other way around. But Dad was gone. Home was gone. And this man wanted to help her, or at least said he did.

"My name's Hilly," she whispered.

"Hilly." He searched her face, and she knew she'd regret this at some point. Dad's words would turn out to be right. You couldn't trust anyone, and strangers would only hurt you.

But, God, she didn't know what else to do right now. She had to trust Cam's kind eyes. This man who knew what to do in a crisis. "My name is Hilly Adams."

## Chapter Five

Thanks to the isolated location, it was tough for the fire department to put the blaze out, but over time they managed. Cam had shrugged off the EMT about four hundred times, but since Laurel was here questioning everyone, the EMT just kept coming back as urged to by his sister.

"I'm fine," he growled when Laurel approached him with the man in tow again.

"You sound like you swallowed glass."

"I'm *fine.*"

Laurel sighed heavily, but nodded toward the EMT, who walked back to the group of first responders huddled around the fire site.

Laurel stood next to him, but her gaze was on Hilly, who sat on a blanket, another draped over her shoulders. The dog was curled up in her lap despite being far too large to be a lapdog.

"She's not talking," Laurel offered.

"She talked. She's just not giving you the answers you want. She doesn't know anything. Not about the fire or the spray paint."

"Dad disappears. A man who doesn't exist on any public record as far as I can tell. Then she hightails it out of the station without telling us much of anything. Her place gets burned down, same day. *Confess* is written on the ground. Ground that's technically on public land and not owned by anyone. You said she was armed to the teeth with enough surveillance equipment to make my department weep with jealousy. She knows something."

"I don't think so." Evidence mattered, sure, but so did a gut feeling. So did the fact Hilly didn't know how to use a phone and had looked absolutely wrecked when she'd told him her name.

"Don't let a pretty face and breasts fool you, Cam," Laurel said, surprising him enough to have him bristling.

Yes, Hilly might be an attractive woman, but as much as he wasn't a cop or detective like his sister, he was former military. He knew a thing or two about reading people.

"I'm taking her home."

"Cam."

"She's a victim in all this, Laurel. I know it. I've dealt with my fair share of victims."

Laurel's expression got pinched, a sure sign she was weakening in her surety that Hilly was a suspect.

"She didn't set the fire herself," Cam added. "Two men. I gave you my descriptions."

"Descriptions that could be anyone." She glanced at the spray paint on the ground. One of her deputies had taken pictures of it at a variety of angles. "She claims she doesn't know any other names her father would go by, and now it looks like we won't be able to find evidence of any."

"Listen to the recording on my phone. I couldn't hear anything, but maybe if you get somewhere quiet it'll tell you something."

"I'll see what we can do with it," Laurel returned. "You know to call if you think of anything else. If she tells you anything else. And I mean *anything*."

"Laurel." It felt like an odd invasion of privacy to reveal what he'd observed regarding Hilly, and yet Cam couldn't help but think it was important. "She didn't know how to use a phone. I think she's been living here, isolated from the world, since she was a little girl."

"Cult?"

"But only the two of them by all accounts."

"Lone-wolf militia type. Weapons and paranoia. It'd fit. I don't know how much infighting goes on in groups like that, but maybe he has some kind of enemy. I'll work with the fire department, look into any similar arson cases, but if these are antigovernment types, profiles or information will be hard to come by. Especially considering his name isn't even in our system." Laurel glanced at Hilly again. "I can't believe she doesn't know more about that. About his fake name or whatever he does." Laurel looked up at him, fierce and determined in the midst of her job. "I need you to convince her working with us is her best option."

"Except if her father is involved in something criminal, that isn't true."

"My job is to find the criminal, Cam."

"But mine isn't."

"I can't believe you," Laurel replied, not even bothering to hide her surprised disgust when she usually kept her emotions firmly under wraps when in uniform.

"You wanted me to help her. Well, I'm helping her. *My* job means keeping clients safe." Usually a client actually asked him to work for them and paid him, but that was just semantics. Hilly *had* offered to pay him, after all.

"I hope for your sake you're right and she doesn't know anything, because it's not going to do your reputation or your business any favors if you end up helping a criminal."

Irritated with a lecture from his younger sister, Cam smirked. "Or is it?"

Laurel huffed and turned away from him, marching back to the group of first responders. He ignored the little sliver of guilt at needling her while she was on duty. She was being short-sighted and too focused on her job, and not thinking about the actual *person* affected by all this.

Cam moved toward Hilly. She couldn't seem to take her eyes off the charred remains of her cabin, but when he approached she spoke.

"You're fighting with your sister?"

"She's just a little frustrated with me. Not unusual when it comes to siblings."

Hilly's eyebrows drew together. "I wouldn't know."

"As the eldest of four, I'm going to assure you, you're very lucky."

Her eyes tracked the scorched, wet remains of her blackened cabin. Yeah, not that lucky. Cam didn't think Hilly Adams knew much about luck.

"Let's go," he offered, nodding toward the huddle of police. "Someone will take me back to my car." He held out his hand to help her up. The dog got to its feet and pushed its head under his hand.

Cam chuckled, petting the happy, friendly dog for a moment before holding his hand out to Hilly again, but she wasn't paying attention to him. She was staring at the remains of her home.

"I don't have anywhere to go," she whispered, gold-brown eyes suspiciously shiny.

"You're going to come home with me," he said firmly.

Her eyes widened and moved to him. "With you?"

"Whether you like it or not, I'm a part of this now. I told you my business is keeping people safe. Consider yourself my business."

She swallowed visibly. "I don't have any choice. I don't have anything. I don't…"

He grabbed her hand and tugged her to her feet. He held her gaze, and he made her a promise he wouldn't allow himself to break. "At the end of all this, you're going to have both."

IT HAD BEEN strange to ride in the police car to the police station. She hadn't been in a car for years. Decades, really. The truck they had moved to the cabin in had broken down when she was ten, and Dad had never felt the need to get another one.

*That you know of.*

She closed her eyes against that ugly voice, a voice that wasn't hers. It was in the whispers and looks of everyone who'd asked her a question today. Deputy Delaney. The earnest young man in a matching uniform to Cam's sister. The firefighters. The paramedic.

Their questions were pointed. Their responses to her answers were judgmental at best. Cam was the only one who talked to her as though he believed her, even though he kept looking at her a little sideways, like she was some fairy creature he was scared to take into the sunlight for fear she might fade away.

But that didn't stop him.

She was in his car. He was driving. It was even weirder than the ride to the police station. She was trusting a stranger, not just to drive her, but to offer her shelter. She was trusting Cam with far too much.

He drove them through a town that looked vaguely familiar. Something about the boardwalk sidewalks and shoved-together buildings that lined Main Street nudged at some long past memory.

Maybe they'd driven through it when they'd moved here. She couldn't remember the name of the town they'd lived in before Dad had moved them to the cabin. Most of her memories before the cabin were fuzzy half memories, but Dad had always spoken as if it was far, far away.

*Is anything Dad told you true?*

Hilly closed her eyes and leaned her forehead against the window. Everything about doubting her father made her feel guilty and sick, and yet he'd allowed this seed of doubt to grow and grow.

*Confess.*

*Confess.*

*Confess.*

"Here we are," Cam murmured.

Hilly opened her eyes. They'd left town behind and were now driving up a curving paved drive. The house at the end was... *Sparkling* was the first word that came to Hilly's mind. *Huge* was the second. Gleaming wood and pristine windows and just acres and acres of wide-open space and mountains.

There was a small cabin in a secluded area a ways away that looked far more like what Hilly was used to.

"This is your house?" she asked. She knew nothing about the outside world, but this kind of extravagance had to mean Cam was important somehow.

"My family's ranch," Cam replied. "Laurel lives in that cabin over there. My brother and I live here with our father. My other sister lives in town, but she comes out and cooks for us quite a bit."

"I don't want to…" She didn't have the vocabulary to explain all the ways this made her uncomfortable. How much she didn't want to go in that house.

"The house has plenty of room for an extra person, as you can see. This is a simple, temporary solution. Where else would you go?"

Somewhere small. Somewhere secluded. Somewhere *safe*.

"I know you don't fully trust me, Hilly."

It was *strange* to hear someone else say her name. Someone other than her father in his rough, gravelly voice.

"But that's okay," Cam was saying. "I don't expect you to trust me yet. You don't have to be comfortable or happy to be here. But I can't exactly let you wander the streets with nothing. We've got an extra room, and Jen or Laurel will spend the night if you're worried about the all-men thing."

"I've only ever lived with a man," Hilly pointed out. Should she be worried about spending the night in a strange house full of men? It seemed no different than spending the night in a strange house full of women. They were all strangers.

"Okay, then."

He parked his truck and Hilly felt as though something sharp had been tied around her, painfully squeezing all the air out. She couldn't breathe. She couldn't... She *couldn't*.

But then Cam's hand rested on hers.

"Breathe. In," he commanded. He waited a beat while she obeyed. "Out."

She followed the orders. It felt like the only sane thing in this whole day. Breathe in. Breathe out. She could breathe. She had to breathe. That made sense.

"You can have as much space or isolation as you need. We'll go inside. I'll show you around. You can hide in your room if you'd feel comfortable, or we can work on the case together."

"The case."

"Laurel and the sheriff's department and fire department will investigate the fire, but your father missing isn't going to be a huge part of that."

"And if it is, my father's the criminal in their scenario," Hilly said. She'd understood that from the questions they'd asked, from the way they'd all looked at her. They believed her father, and to an extent her, were criminals.

"It's true. You were living on public land, Hilly. The name not existing. The fire. 'Confess.' You have to admit, it doesn't look good to an outsider."

Except she didn't understand outsiders. She couldn't remember the last time she'd had an interaction with a human aside from her father prior to today. There'd been more people before they'd moved here, but Hilly didn't remember anyone in particular.

It had been her, Dad and the animals.

*Confess.*

"But this is where it's rather handy I followed you home," Cam said, and she realized even though her breathing had evened out his hand was still on hers. "I'm not law enforcement, Hilly. I don't need to decide if your father is a criminal or not. I only have to find him for you."

"I can't pay you now. My money is…gone." Everything was gone.

Cam shrugged, even though she knew people on the outside didn't do anything without payment. Dad had always told her that. During the few rebellions she'd entertained long ago she'd threatened to run away. Dad had always explained she'd never get anywhere without money, and back then he'd always kept the cash hidden. It had only been as an adult that he'd trusted her enough with some things.

But never leaving. Never with the outside world.

Dad was right in one thing. These people had made her doubt him. His intentions, his past, everything she knew about him.

Or had his longer-than-normal disappearance done that?

"Come inside," Cam urged gently. "Let's get something to eat. We'll need to figure out a place for Free to stay."

"With me. She has to stay with me."

Cam made an odd face, but then he nodded. "All right. With you." He pushed the driver's-side door open, then pulled the seat forward so Free could jump out of the back. Hilly pushed her own door open and stepped out of the truck.

The air was cold and somehow different than the air she was used to. It wasn't as heavy. The trees were all far away, and the mountains were majestic points on the horizon. Everything was *open* and vast.

She was enthralled by it all, but in the midst of this expanse of land around her was a looming house she didn't even want to look at, let alone step inside. Everything about the house was intimidating, from the size to the clean way it shone in the fiery sunset. It was almost as if mud and grime didn't dare touch this place. She didn't like it. Didn't trust it. She wanted to stay outside, but it was silly to want that.

She was lucky. If Cam hadn't been there, she'd be alone and with nothing. Though she wasn't sure she completely trusted him, he hadn't orchestrated that fire or the law enforcement presence. He hadn't written "confess" on her yard. Whoever he was, he was separate from this strange thing happening to her and her father.

And he was the only one who wouldn't vilify her father unnecessarily. At least, he said he wouldn't. She was too tired, and, yes, hungry, to worry about if he was lying about that or not.

She didn't have a choice.

But Cam had said at the end of this she'd have one, and that was what she wanted. That was what she'd work toward. She needed to start thinking ahead instead of circling unproductive thoughts and worries.

She glanced at Cam. He was standing on the porch now, Free at his heels, waiting for her to follow. He didn't push. He stayed there and let her look around, let her come to her own conclusions.

Trust or not, she liked that.

"What will you need to find my father?"

"A picture would be the best start."

"I need some paper and a pencil then. I don't have any actual photos, but I can draw okay." She moved forward, and noted his patient expression had morphed into something like confusion. Or maybe suspicion.

Neither mattered. Only one thing did. She met Cam on the porch, held his dark gaze. "I need to find him. I can't do it alone. I need your help, regardless of trust."

Cam nodded, then led her inside.

# Chapter Six

Cam didn't know what to do with this woman. At turns she was lost and completely vulnerable, and then she just pulled herself together and marched on.

She wanted paper and a pencil. So, he led her to the kitchen and pointed to a seat at the table, then gathered the supplies she'd requested.

She settled herself at the table, and when he handed her the materials, she immediately got to work, Free curling up at her feet.

Dad would be pissed about the dog in the house, but Cam felt he didn't care as much as he once would have. Last Christmas, his father's affair with a married woman had come to light, and it had changed Cam's estimation of his father immensely.

A man who talked about right and wrong, good and bad, who then secretly slept with another man's wife—a woman who was part of the family Delaneys had looked down upon and been feuding with since the dawn of Bent... Well, he was not the man Cam had thought he was.

But Dad was out of town and Cam's relationship with his father wasn't important. What was important was Hilly.

"You don't have to do this all now. You're probably hungry."

She shook her head, furiously scribbling. "This first."

Cam had to admit he didn't hold out much hope for a usable sketch, but if it gave her some sense of focus, it wasn't so bad to let her have at it.

They both reeked of smoke and would need showers. At least he was starting to overcome the stinging shards-of-glass feeling in his throat enough to want to eat.

Dylan would be home soon from the bank, and Cam had called Jen to come cook them dinner once she closed up the store. Though he hadn't asked Laurel over, he wouldn't put it past her to stop by just to poke at things for her case.

Cam needed to do some of his own poking first. "You don't know how to use a phone." He winced at how abrasive that came out.

But Hilly didn't even look up as she focused on her drawing. "We didn't have one."

"Not even a cell?"

"Dad didn't trust the outside world."

"Why?"

She looked up at him, her expressive mouth turning downward and her dark eyebrows drawing together. "I don't know why exactly. Lots of reasons. You can't trust people. They'll only hurt you. Staying away is safe. Out here..." She looked around the spacious, well-kept kitchen. "Not safe at all."

"But you are here."

"Like I said before, I don't have a choice." She flipped over the paper and then started writing something.

Cam heard the front door squeak open and then click shut. Jen breezed in. "You sounded urgent on the phone so I got Lydia to come close the store for me." She wrinkled her nose at Cam. "You *stink*."

"Fires will do that to you."

Jen's lips firmed. "It isn't bad enough you had to go risking your life as a Marine, now you're in the middle of fires. You and Laurel just can't seem to keep yourselves out of trouble, can you?" She took a few steps and hefted some bags onto the counter, then she turned to Hilly, all smiles.

"Hi. I'm Jen Delaney."

"H-hi. I'm…" She trailed off, flicking a glance at Cam. She looked lost, and it did something uncomfortable to his chest. Made it too tight and reminded him of helpless feelings he'd hoped to leave behind when he'd left the military.

She didn't know whether or not to give her name. She thought the outside world was dangerous and she had no choice but to weather it.

"This is Hilly. Who also stinks."

Both women gave him outraged looks, but Hilly's mouth quirked a little bit, the reaction he'd intended to elicit.

"Well, I'll start on some dinner," Jen said, clearly determined to take charge. "Why don't you show our guest where she can get cleaned up?"

"Oh, I—"

Cam crossed to the table and took her elbow lightly. "You can finish the drawing later."

Hilly clutched the paper as he tugged her to her feet. She glanced back at Jen, then at the hallway Cam was leading her toward. Free followed them, her claws clicking against the hardwood floor.

"I only have these clothes." Hilly swallowed, and it dawned on him she didn't just mean *here*, she meant at all. All her clothes and things had burned up. She was taking it like a champ, but he'd let himself forget her whole life had just burned to the ground.

"I'll find something for you to change into. Whatever you need in the next few days, you only have to ask."

She shoved the paper at him. "It isn't perfect, but it might help."

He led her to the staircase and up the stairs as he studied the picture. It was a million times better than anything he could draw. While it was a long shot he could find anyone her father had run into, this picture was a tangible thing he could show people.

"Hilly, this is amazing."

"I wrote everything he was wearing, anything he'd have on him, and hair and eye color on the back," she said, clasping and unclasping her hands as she followed him down another hallway.

"This'll be a good start," he said hoping to ease some of those nerves that were now vibrating off her.

She needed things to do. She needed to focus on the next step instead of all the losses she was in the middle of.

That he knew firsthand.

He stopped at the bathroom door and nudged it open. "Here's the bathroom. Wait right here."

Her eyes widened a bit, but she stood rooted to the spot as he walked farther down the hallway and went into his room. He dropped the picture on his bed, then rummaged around in his closet looking for a robe or something like it. He thought he maybe had one he'd been given as a gift at some point or another.

Once Hilly was in the shower he'd ask Jen if she had any clothes he could pawn off on Hilly, but he wanted to get Hilly settled into a shower first.

Finally he found the robe he was pretty sure he'd never worn, then he returned to the bathroom, where she stood looking like she hadn't moved a muscle. The fear and the nerves were all back with a vengeance and he wished he had some way to take it all away from her, but it would require time.

He handed her the robe, and then stepped inside the bathroom and opened the little closet there.

"Towels in here. Soap and whatever in the shower itself," he said, pointing toward the glass stall. "Feel free to poke around for anything you need. It should be pretty well stocked. Between me and my brother, and

Laurel, Gracie and Jen coming and going, we usually have plenty of stuff at the ready."

"I thought you only had two sisters."

"Yes. Gracie's my cousin. She lived with us for a while. She lives in town now, but there was some trouble a while back. Well, anyway, long boring history. You go ahead and clean up." He stepped out of the bathroom and gestured her in.

She took a few hesitant steps into the bathroom, looking around wide-eyed before her gaze returned to him. "Where will you be?"

She didn't trust him, but he was still her safe place. She didn't know this house or his sister, but in an odd way she knew *him*.

He walked over to the door to the guest bedroom. He shoved it open. "I'm going to be in here getting things ready for you. Door open. You just come in here when you're done, and if I'm not here, trust I'll be back shortly."

She nodded, clutching the robe to her chest. "Okay. Okay." She chewed on her lip, but then straightened and closed the door, determination etched into the features of her face before the door clicked shut.

Cam let out a breath. For a second he allowed himself to consider how completely out of his depth he was. His plan had been a quiet security business, not fires and investigations that might run counter to his sister's law enforcement ones. His plan had definitely not been a vulnerable woman who, by all accounts, didn't have a clue as to how the "outside world" worked.

But she was his responsibility. He'd decided that, and if he could help her…if he could help… Well, things would be better. They'd have to be.

THE HOT WATER didn't seem to run out, once she'd figured out how to get it going in the first place. The sheer heat of it was the one thing Hilly couldn't get over. Dad had sometimes spoken of the extravagance of the outside world, so while this house was like an unfamiliar land, it wasn't totally foreign in idea. Some people needed fancy things and too big of a space to convince themselves they were better than others, Dad always said.

But she hadn't expected there to be *so much* to that. Space and nice wood, sure. But the endless hot water was a marvel. Sweet-smelling soaps and shampoos that left her feeling soft instead of scrubbed raw. Towels, she noted as she dried off, that had more luxury than any of her clothes. Mirrors to stare at a face that wasn't altogether familiar.

She dried herself off watching the face in the mirror. What did Cam see when he looked at her? His sister had swept into the kitchen all smiles and chatter and Hilly had felt like some...wounded creature all of a sudden.

She supposed it didn't really matter what he saw. It didn't particularly matter what *she* saw. What a person looked like didn't matter. It was what they did and what they said that mattered.

Cam had done and said all the right things so far. He was kind. She had to believe he was kind or she'd go a little crazy.

*And he looks very nice on top of that.*

She shook her head at the ridiculous thought and pulled on the robe. The fabric was plush and velvety. It dwarfed her completely.

It was awkward to step out into the hallway in the too-big robe, naked underneath. It covered her entirely, but that didn't change her knowledge of not having underwear on. Not wearing socks.

She tiptoed to the open door Cam had pointed out earlier. It was foolish to *sneak* and yet her brain and body couldn't get on the same page. He was in the room, staring out the window, the side of his face to her.

Something about that profile, strong and

focused, sharp and chiseled, made her stomach swoop and her heart pick up an extra beat. She'd never experienced this strange sensation before, but only Cam seemed to bring it out in her. Her reaction to his sisters, to the firefighters, to everyone else was far more…scared. Timid. She wanted to hide.

Cam didn't make her want to hide.

Free got up from her spot lying at his feet, which alerted Cam to Hilly's presence. He turned to face her, mouth opened as if to speak.

But he froze, his mouth staying open while his eyebrows raised. Then he blinked and the weird shock of his expression was gone. "This is your room for now. Jen found you some clothes. I don't know if they'll fit, but I'll let you sort through all that. I'll wait just outside, then we can go downstairs and eat."

Hilly nodded and Cam quickly strode out of the room, closing the door behind him. There had been a tenseness in him she didn't understand.

But understanding Cam, or even her reaction to him, was hardly important right now. She *was* hungry, and she wanted Cam to start looking into the picture she'd drawn and hopefully use it to get some clue as to where Dad could be.

She pulled on the soft pants that were a little too big, but had a tie she could use to keep them up. Once they were fastened, she dropped the robe and pulled on a sweatshirt. It should be strange to wear someone else's clothes, but they were so much softer and warmer and cleaner than her own. It was a weird kind of relief.

There weren't any socks, or anything to pull her hair back with. She'd have to ask Cam for some. It lodged something a lot more uncomfortable in her gut than that swooping feeling from looking at Cam. She didn't want to have to ask for things.

*You take care of yourself, Hilly. Don't trust anyone to take care of anything for you. You are your only real friend.*

She should have understood that every time Dad said that, he didn't mean they were a team. She'd thought they were in it together against the world. She should have realized long before now what he meant was she was alone.

Period.

Now she was alone without her father, without a home, without *anything*. It was horrifying, but it meant… It meant she had to trust herself. Her words. Not Dad's. He'd disappeared on her.

She only had herself now.

She marched over to the door and jerked it open. "I need socks," she stated.

Cam was waiting in the hallway and he certainly looked surprised by her unnecessarily loud statement, but he nodded. "Follow me. I'll get you some of mine."

She followed him down the hallway to a room at the end. He stepped in and immediately went for a dresser.

The room was big. Almost bigger than the cabin.

*Your no-longer-existing cabin.*

But everything had a careful neatness that made it feel way less lived-in than her cluttered room, and her ramshackle home.

*Gone. All gone.*

She swallowed down the lump in her throat. She wouldn't cry. Not now. There was too much to do, and Dad always said…

*To hell with what Dad said.*

Cam pressed a pair of socks into her palm as he enclosed her hands and the socks in his. He squeezed gently. "Laurel's coming over. She said she listened to the recording my phone took. Maybe she has some leads."

Hilly nodded, which was when she realized a few tears had escaped because they trickled down her cheeks. She took a deep, shaky breath. She should feel embarrassed, but she didn't. Cam was offering her comfort and focus, and that was nice.

"You need food. We both do."

It was then she realized he'd showered, too. He was wearing different clothes and though she could still smell the faint smell of smoke on both of them, there was something piney and clean on top of it now.

This place had two showers with endless hot water and endless rooms, and how on earth had she landed here?

She followed him back down the endless halls and huge staircase, and even Free at her side didn't make her feel safe. She thought the house might swallow her up if she let it. So, she focused on Cam. On how broad his shoulders were compared to hers. On how most of his hair seemed dry, but there was a little wet patch in the very center of the back of his head making his brown hair darker there.

When he walked her back into the kitchen, which now smelled like something foreign but delicious, not only was Jen there, but so was Laurel.

She still wore her uniform, and she looked strong. Jen was soft and like...like a woman. Laurel was strong and was a kind of woman Hilly understood a little better, but then the uniform went and undercut any camaraderie Hilly might have felt.

"Anything on the file?" Cam asked, looking over Jen's shoulder at what she was cooking until she slapped him away.

Cam grinned. Laurel rolled her eyes.

Hilly felt like running far, far away. She'd never been in a room with three other people before. Unless she counted dogs as people.

"We didn't get much," Laurel said, answering Cam's question as she leaned against the kitchen counter behind her. "But there were two names mentioned. Ethan was one, and it wasn't clear if it was a first or last name, but he was one of the men there."

All eyes turned to Hilly, but she didn't know anyone by that name. She didn't like three pairs of eyes on her. Panic clawed at her throat and she just stood there, immobile.

"What was the other name?" Cam asked, crossing his arms over his chest. He looked very formidable. She was glad he was on her side.

*Are you sure he's on your side?*

But he moved forward, and then let his arms fall. He pulled a chair back from the table and nudged her into it. Free laid her head on Hilly's leg in someone else's clothes, but the dog looking at her hoping for a pet eased something.

"At first we thought they were saying Hilly," Laurel said. Her expression was blank as she continued. "But the syllables weren't right. They were talking about a woman named Hillary."

Something cold and sharp skittered up Hilly's spine. Laurel and Cam's similar dark eyes watching her with speculation didn't help the feeling any.

"Is that your full name?"

Hilly shook her head, but her vision had gone topsy-turvy and her stomach felt upended. "No. Hilly. Just Hilly. Always Hilly."

But she could hear someone's low, calm voice saying Hillary. It ached, that voice. She didn't know why. It was all in her head, but she could *hear* it. Like a memory, but too foggy for that. A bad dream. A bad dream was all.

"Hilly," Cam said, his voice low and forceful. She clung to that force.

*Never trust an outsider, Hilly. They'll only hurt you.*

"Are you sure your full name isn't Hillary?"

But she wasn't. She wasn't sure about anything anymore.

## Chapter Seven

Cam hated the way Hilly's determined strength would randomly desert her, and all that fear and uncertainty radiated in wide eyes. Free must have sensed it, too, because she whimpered a little and licked Hilly's hand.

It seemed to center Hilly back on what they were talking about. She scratched the dog behind the ears, keeping her gaze on the dog's head. "I can't prove that to you. But I only ever remember being called Hilly."

"There are a lot of holes in your stories," Laurel said.

Cam shot her a silencing look, but she paid him no mind. She was in cop mode.

"Not holes so much as things I don't know, I'd say," Hilly replied, steel in her tone.

Cam felt an odd swelling of pride at the fact she wouldn't back down to Laurel's too-hard questioning.

"Well, we'll do a search on Hillary Adams, unless you have any other aliases you'd like to tell us about?"

"Laurel. Enough."

"It's fine, Cam," Hilly said, but it was clearly not fine as she'd stopped petting Free and instead had white-knuckled hands fisted in her lap. "It's just like you said to me. She has no reason to trust me. It doesn't make anything I've said a lie. Or an omission."

"So, as far as you know, your name is Hilly Adams?"

Hilly took a deep breath, but her eyes blazed with fury, just like when she'd pointed the gun at him earlier today. "Yes."

"And your birthday is?"

"July 4."

"How long have you been living in the cabin?"

"I was five or six when we moved there, so almost twenty years. We'd lived in a town before that, but I can't remember much except bits and pieces about the house."

"You asked her all these questions before," Cam said through gritted teeth.

"She's checking to make sure I can keep my stories straight," Hilly said loftily. "I might have been isolated, but I'm not stupid."

"This would go a lot easier if you both

stopped treating me like I'm the enemy," Laurel said. "I'm trying to find a lead here, and Hilly's right about a few things. Namely, we have no reason to trust each other. No hard feelings. I'm collecting facts."

Cam knew it was Laurel's job and all, but it didn't help with his irritation. He wasn't sure it helped with Hilly's either, but she smoothed out her features.

"I don't have anything to confess," Hilly said calmly, concisely. "I don't know of anything my father would have to confess. We live off the grid. We have for almost as long as I can remember. If there's no record of him, I can't help you. I assume if there's no record of me, it's for the same reason."

"A distrust of government?"

Hilly's eyebrows drew together. "I'm not sure. I suppose you could say that. He told me not to trust anyone outside our clearing. It wasn't government focused."

"And you never left that cabin or clearing?"

"No. We foraged or hunted in the woods sometimes, but I was never allowed to go far. The police station was the first time I'd been out of that clearing in almost twenty years."

She said that so calmly, as if it was perfectly normal. Cam supposed if you'd been conditioned to think so for twenty years, you would believe that. Still, it ate away at him, that people could just be secreted away right under all their noses.

"What about school?" Laurel asked.

"I was homeschooled. I don't have a certificate or anything because Dad didn't want any record, but we did everything up through a high school diploma."

"Doctor?"

Hilly shook her head. "We didn't get sick or injured often, but we just patched each other up when we did. Dad had all sorts of books and medical supplies."

When it dawned on her everything she'd lost, her shoulders slumped. Over and over again. What amazed Cam was that she just kept straightening them back up.

"You don't know of anyone, I mean *anyone*, who would have had any contact with your father?"

"I told you. All his interaction with the outside world was done far away from me. No one came to our cabin. He always left to do whatever business he did. I thought it was trading pelts or meat for supplies."

"But it wasn't?"

Hilly looked helplessly at Laurel. "I don't know. I don't know. It just seems like maybe there was more to it *now*, but at the time?" She glanced at Cam, that helplessness still there.

He was about to order Laurel away, demand she give Hilly some breathing room, when Laurel pushed away from the counter. "All right. Well, we'll look into the names on the tape. See what we can come up with. I'll undoubtedly have more questions for you."

"Great," Hilly muttered.

"Cam?" Laurel nodded toward the door where she was headed. He followed her to the entryway before she spoke.

"The fire department will handle the fire investigation and cooperate with us on ours. But I can't do much on that end until the fire inspector goes through the debris. He's on his way, but I doubt he'll get much done in the dark. Like I told Hilly, we'll search the names, get her drawing out there and I'll cross check Adams with some of the militia groups around here."

"You're still thinking antigovernment?"

"It looks that way." Laurel rubbed a hand over her jaw, some of that calm cop mask slipping so he could see the frustration underneath. "Doesn't make much sense, all this, and that's grating. Because by all accounts it's just the two of them, not some organized group. But a Fourth of July birthday. The

Adams last name that might be fake. A dog named Free—Dad'll hate that dog in here, by the way. That's a lot of patriotism stuff. But he could be a very lone wolf, and any groups could be a very dead end."

"That could be where he goes. Group meetings or whatever. Maybe he wanted to keep her out of it and that's why she didn't think he had any specific animosity toward the government."

"Possible. She might be connected to this, though, even if she doesn't know it. What kind of parent keeps their child completely hidden away? No school, no records. No *doctor*. She could be the thing he was trying to hide."

*Confess.* Cam was sure that spray-painted word had to do with Hilly's father, but people used children to get to their parents all the time. She could be the thing they were after, especially if Laurel was right and she was the thing being hidden. "We need to take some precautions. They could be after her for any reason."

"I'll assign someone to the house."

"You know as well as I do one deputy isn't going to keep this big spread safe."

"And you know as well as I do Bent County can't afford more." Laurel sighed, and he knew that fact weighed on her even if she tried to keep her cop mask firmly in place. "Especially without more information."

Information. It gave Cam an idea. An idea his sister would really hate, so he didn't plan on sharing it with her. "Don't bother with the one deputy then. I was a former Marine. I'm supposed to be starting a security business. I'll handle it."

Laurel frowned. "You're up to something."

"Just some supersneaky security business that's likely not quite on your up-and-up. I'll spare you the details for your professional integrity."

She scowled at him, but she didn't prod. "I'll likely be back tomorrow with questions. If you could both be less antagonistic, that'd be great."

"Sure thing, sis."

She rolled her eyes and strode out the front door. Cam locked it behind her and smiled. Her questions wouldn't make him antagonistic tomorrow, because he and Hilly would be gone tomorrow.

If Laurel needed information, the best way to find it was to go after it.

HILLY HAD NEVER had a meal that tasted so good. She considered herself a fair cook, but what she made for her and Dad never turned out like this. It might have something to do with the ingredients, but she figured Jen had a talent for it, as well.

She preferred to focus on the food rather than the fact she was at the table with three other people. Cam, Jen and their brother Dylan, whose palpable intensity might have unnerved her if it didn't remind her so much of Cam.

The three of them chatted, and Hilly could barely follow it all. Dad didn't talk much, and when he did it wasn't so much of a conversation. Usually he was instructing her. She'd never thought of that as a negative, as a lack of something, but there was such a warmth between these three.

It didn't make any sense to her, and it set her even more on edge than she was. She didn't belong here. She didn't belong anywhere now that the cabin was gone.

She surreptitiously looked at Cam to find his dark, steady gaze on her. It made her stomach jitter and her cheeks feel hot. It made her want to run away.

But she felt rooted to the spot.

"You've had a long day," he said, somehow sounding casual despite that foreign intensity in his gaze. "We should get a good night's sleep."

"I'll clean up," Jen said, smiling comfortingly at Hilly. "And if you need anything, just let me know." Jen looked down at Free. "You, too, puppy."

Hilly didn't know what to do with all this kindness. She attempted a smile and muttered a thanks before Cam was ushering her back up to the room he'd shown her earlier, Free at their heels.

"I don't understand all this," she muttered.

"All what exactly?"

"Why you're all so nice."

Cam shrugged. "We don't exactly have a reason to be mean. I know Laurel was rough on you, but she wants to do good. Help people. It's a kind of ingrained Delaney trait, let's say."

"Is Dylan in the military, too?" It would make sense. He held himself almost identically to Cam, even if he had a slightly slicker polish to him.

"Oh, no. He's a bank manager, but there's a code. A code that comes with being a Delaney in Bent," Cam explained, walking into the room that would be hers while he and his siblings were *helping people*. "You do the right thing. You help people when you can. Well, as long as they aren't Carson people."

"Who are Carson people?"

"It's complicated. Basically Bent was built by two families. The Delaneys, law-abiding and wanting to do right, and the Carsons. Who were usually thieving outlaws."

Hilly didn't know what to do with that. "What does your dad do?" she asked. She couldn't picture this big, broad, *intense* man having parents to boss him around.

Cam stopped moving because he was standing in the middle of the room, but there was a tenseness that crept into his muscles that she didn't understand.

"I'll take Free out, then come back with some things," he announced.

Which was odd. Free probably did need to go out, but why hadn't he suggested that when they'd been downstairs? "I can take her out."

Cam shook his head. "I want you to stay put. Fact of the matter is, those men who burned down your place might have been looking for you."

"Clearly they didn't know I was there."

"That doesn't mean they don't know you exist. Or didn't see us escaping. We just don't know. So we'll play it safe."

"Then why do *you* get to go?"

His mouth curved, and the thing that fluttered in her stomach was too strong to be butterflies. It was like tiny jabs from a miniature boxer. "I've got a little more experience in protecting myself."

"I shot you."

"Yes, you did. But you didn't mean to, and you barely hurt me. I'm just fine now." He slapped his palm to his thigh. "Come on, Free."

Her dog—*her* dog—happily trotted after Cam as he strode away.

Hilly frowned and surveyed the room. Everything about it made her uncomfortable. The floors gleamed. The bedsheets were a blinding, feminine white. The curtains were lace. She felt like she'd dirty anything just by touching it.

On a sigh, she slowly lowered herself onto the edge of the bed. She nearly moaned. Everything was soft, reminding her that the heavy feeling dogging her limbs was probably exhaustion—physical and emotional.

She eyed the pillows at the top of the bed. Faint pink flowers dotted the fabric. Not faint after years of use and hard washing, but a purposeful light color that matched the walls.

Maybe she should think of this all as a dream. If she crawled into this pretty, sinfully comfortable bed and fell asleep, she'd wake back up in her lumpy mattress in a non–burned down cabin.

Tears stung her eyes but she blinked them away. She couldn't think about home and all she'd lost. So she ruthlessly pulled back the covers and slid her body in between them.

It was like heaven. Soft. Clean. She could barely smell the smoke that clung to her hair despite the multiple washings she'd given it in the shower with some fruity-smelling shampoo.

She didn't allow herself to lie down. Instead she moved the pillows behind her back and sat there, leaning against the headboard.

She heard Free coming and then, in a blur, the dog happily jumped right onto the bed. Hilly winced.

"Don't worry about it," Cam said, opening the computer he'd brought in. He pulled a small chair from the desk in the corner next to the bed. It was too small and dainty for him, but it didn't collapse when he sat on it like she'd expected it to.

So he was sitting next to her. While she was in a bed.

She was a very sheltered woman. Had never had anyone but her father in the room when she'd been in bed. No other relatives, especially with relationships like the ones the Delaneys seemed to have.

Heat prickled along her skin. It wasn't embarrassment exactly. She knew that feeling. This was something more complicated, and something to do with the fact that Cam was a man.

And she was a woman.

She'd read books. Dad had some old Westerns he'd occasionally let her read for fun. Men and women did interesting things in beds. Things she'd always wanted to know more about, and never had the opportunity to explore—fictionally or in reality.

Funny, Cam could fit into the pages of one of those books. He didn't dress like a cowboy, but there was a kind of swagger about him. A certainty. A confidence.

She shifted in the bed, trying to figure out how to get comfortable. Comfortable was probably a pipe dream with Cam this close to her.

He angled his computer screen toward her. "Laurel has a theory about something your father may have been involved in."

"My father's a good man," Hilly said. All Cam's talk about Delaneys and their goodness had given her a certain kind of defensiveness.

Her father was good. She was upset he'd left her because she knew the most likely reason was he was hurt somewhere. Or worse.

She wished the perfect white linens would swallow her whole, or at least let her sleep until this mess was sorted.

"I'm not saying he isn't," Cam said gently. "Based on your name, your birthday and the cabin on public land, it adds up to certain kinds of groups that are antigovernment."

"Why would July the Fourth and Adams mean he's *anti*government? Wouldn't that be the opposite?"

"They're anti current government. Bureaucracy. A lot of these groups want to go back to some fictionalized version of the past where things were good and men were men."

Hilly frowned because that *did* sound like something Dad would say. He idolized the past. Frontiersmen and the Wild West.

"I just want to look through information about a few of the local groups like that, and see if anything rings any bells for you."

His dark eyes were focused on the screen. He was a man on a mission. She didn't understand why he'd taken up the mantle of *her* mission, but maybe like the bed she just needed to accept it.

Her life was in literal ashes. Why not take whatever non-destroyed things came her way?

Cam scrolled through pages, reading things aloud, asking her questions. It mainly just gave her a headache.

Until he opened a website to a group called the Protectors. Their symbol was one she was very, very familiar with.

She felt that same cold, sharp tingle in her spine as when Laurel had said the name Hillary. Hillary.

"Dad has this tattoo," she whispered.

Cam's eyes sharpened on her. "What?"

"The eagle. With the gun in its talons. He has it tattooed on his back." Hilly reached back and touched the spot on her own. "Right beneath the shoulder blade. I haven't seen it often, but enough to know that's it."

Cam's gaze returned to the screen. "All right. Then that's the plan."

"What's the plan?"

"We need to know what they know. We need to know how your father connects to them, since he clearly does. So, we go to them."

Hilly looked at the screen. There was a picture of five men with guns, one exactly like Dad had. They all wore bandannas over the bottom half of their faces and sunglasses over their eyes.

"Somehow I don't think they'll be very forthcoming."

"No. Which is why we won't be going as ourselves. We're going to pretend we want to join."

Hilly blinked at him. "We are?"

Cam kept talking, though most of his concentration was clearly on the website he was scanning. "And we have to act fast. I can't risk Laurel finding out what we're going to do. She wouldn't approve. Or worse, she'd want police involvement."

"That'd be worse?"

"For now. What we need is information. The best way to get information from people is to act like you want to be one of them. So, we'll want to be one of them."

"We?" she asked again, because he was... including her.

She'd never been included.

He looked up at her, studying her face in that way that made her blush. "Well, you have a choice. You can come with me and try to help me figure it out, or you can stay here. Jen would take good care of you, and you'd be safe. I'd certainly feel better if you were safe, and coming with me is dangerous, but you have to make that decision for yourself, because you're the one who has to live with it."

"You're giving me a choice."

"It is your life on the line, Hilly."

Her life. *Her* life. It had never been her life before, on the line or otherwise. Which made her decision for her. "When do we leave?"

## Chapter Eight

He'd told Hilly to sleep while he got ready. He packed clothes, including some of Jen's for Hilly, supplies and food. Free had followed him around as he gathered everything and stowed it into two backpacks.

He'd decided to bring the dog. It would add to his story of a young couple searching for the kind of freedom a group like the Protectors offered.

He'd feel a little better if he could leave Hilly behind and do this kind of recon mission himself, but he didn't trust Laurel not to press her too hard. Hilly would be more protected at his side, anyway, and a woman and a dog would add to his credibility. And since she was the only one who knew anything about her father, he had to use her.

There was always the possibility Hilly's dad was in the group and would recognize her and blow their cover, but so far Hilly hadn't said anything that led him to believe her father wished her harm.

Cam also wasn't sure he could believe the man Hilly described would full-on abandon her like he had. *If* Hilly's father was hurt, or worse, they needed to find that out as soon as possible. Hopefully, so they could help him.

As much as he respected Laurel as a cop and a detective, her loyalty was to the law and the sheriff's department, like his had once been to the Marines. It was limiting, and it often left you unable to help people in an immediate way. So much so that you got to a point that you forgot that you *could* help people. And you failed your friends.

He shook that thought away and focused on the task at hand. Based on the information he'd gleaned from the Protectors website, Facebook group page and some message boards he'd had to deep-dive to find, he had a little bit of an idea where the compound was.

So, Jen was going to drop them off up at the state park. There'd be a trail for a while, but then he'd have to use his old Eagle Scout skills to orienteer his way to the potential compound.

By his calculations, it'd be a day or two hike to the location—three, tops, if the information was a little off. He could handle that no problem, and considering Hilly had lived off-grid for most of her life, he imagined she could, too. Still, he'd made sure her pack was lighter than his.

Jen drove them through pre-dawn dark to the state park. When they arrived and got out of the car, he quickly shrugged on his pack, then helped Hilly with hers. He made sure the straps fit around her at the right spots.

The coat Jen had found Hilly was a pinch too big, so Cam didn't feel too self-conscious about adjusting her straps. She was so buried under the fabric there was no chance of accidentally...

His fingers fumbled on the strap, but he hurried up tightening it for her and moved to his sister.

"Be careful," Jen said, clearly fretting. "And don't tell me Marines are always careful."

He grinned at her. "We'll be fine. As long as you don't tip Laurel off."

Jen wrinkled her nose. "I don't know why I'm always the go-to when it comes to lying to Laurel."

"Because you're the only one brave enough to do it," he said, giving Jen's arm a squeeze. "Give us time."

"I hope you know what you're doing."

When she turned to Hilly, the nerves and uncertainty had been wiped off her face. "Good luck, Hilly."

Hilly's mouth curved. He couldn't characterize it as a smile, though on the surface it looked like one. Still, she looked that way at Jen and Dylan with every interaction. A discomfort lingered on the edges, in the wary cast of her eyes.

She looked at him like that, too, though not quite as much or as carefully. He wanted to find a way to eradicate it completely, to coax a real smile out of Hilly.

Which was not his mission. His mission was finding her father and hopefully, as a result, the people who'd burned down her cabin. The Protectors was the best shot he had at getting an idea of where the man might go when he wasn't with Hilly. He might even be with them.

*That* was the only thing he could focus on. Not golden-brown eyes, with or without wariness. Jen got back in her car and drove away and Cam pulled out his map. He'd already shown Hilly his plan, but it didn't hurt to go over it again.

"We'll start at this path. Once we reach this curve here, we'll veer off. You've got water and snacks in your pack, but we'll need to be careful of wildlife, especially bears. If you need a rest—"

"I know I wasn't a Marine or anything, but I can handle bear protocol and eating my own snack."

Cam smiled sheepishly. "Sorry. I'm used to giving all the orders or none at all. Middle Ground is not my middle name."

That got a bit of a chuckle out of her. "Let's get started, then."

Cam nodded and led the way. The path was narrow, so Hilly followed behind, Free behind her.

A pretty spring morning began to dawn. Cold, but sunny. It would be warm this afternoon. Hopefully snow or rain would hold off until they reached the compound.

"Did you do a lot of hiking in the military?" Hilly asked.

"Some."

"What about pretending to be someone you're not and infiltrating small groups of potentially dangerous men?"

He hadn't been very comfortable discussing his Marine days with his family since he'd been back, but Hilly's question didn't set him on edge. Maybe because it was more about what they were doing here and now than what he'd done before. "Some of that, too."

"Is it worth it? Seeing the world? I never had much inclination to. I like…liked my cabin. Liked my life, but you know what I really liked?"

"What?"

"Sleeping in that very nice bed last night."

He chuckled, charmed by her simple enjoyment. Still, he took her question seriously. "I'm not sure I've seen the parts of the world most people desire to travel to. I think there's something special in realizing the world is so vastly different. The geography, the customs, the challenges—and yet at the end of the day we're all people. And we all have homes. I was happy to come home to mine."

"If you liked home so much, why did you join the military?"

"I wanted to help people."

"Right."

"You don't trust my help." It bothered him. An itch he couldn't find the location of. No matter how much he knew it didn't matter. He could help her whether she trusted it or not. He also didn't *have* to trust her.

But here they were.

"I am following you deep into the woods," Hilly said, sounding resigned. "I'm not sure what I feel is a lack of trust."

"Then what is it?"

"I know I'm not supposed to trust anyone. The fact that I do? It would be like…if you were a vegetarian your whole life and then ate a piece of meat and discovered it was delicious."

"I'm surprised you know what a vegetarian is."

"I might not have much interaction with people, but I've read anything Dad let me gets my hands on. Including cookbooks. I could make you a hearty vegetarian chili if you're interested."

"Rain check," Cam offered good-naturedly.

Free barked and Cam looked back at the dog.

"Probably just a—"

But Free barked again and then took off, racing into the trees, Hilly immediately taking off after her.

Which meant he had to, as well.

"Free! Stop! Halt! Free!" It was no use. Free was so fast, so determined, and she was nearly out of sight no matter how hard Hilly ran. Hilly panted with the exertion of it all, panic beating through her body.

She couldn't lose Free, too. She couldn't. Free was very good at following commands for the most part. She didn't run off.

"Free!"

"We can track her."

Hilly nearly tripped over a log at Cam's voice. She'd been running so hard she hadn't realized he was so close to her. He put an arm on her shoulder, clearly wanting her to stop running.

But Free was all she had left. She couldn't lose her dog.

"We'll track her," Cam said, his voice calm and clear. He'd had to run as well to catch up with her so quickly and yet he wasn't even winded. "We'll find her. Maybe she's leading us to something."

Hilly nodded, trying to believe it. She felt moisture on her face, but she was sure it was just her eyes watering from running through the cold air, not tears. The crushing pain in her chest was from the run, not from this re-curring feeling everything was being taken away from her.

She sniffled as Cam knelt down. "See? It's nice and muddy. We'll be able to follow her path. Come on."

"What if we get lost?" Hilly managed, ir-ritated with herself when her voice came out wobbly.

Cam pulled out his map as he stood. He studied the paper, then his compass. He wasted precious time until Hilly was all but vibrating with nerves.

"Right," Cam said with such certainty some of those nerves eased. He shoved both items back into his coat pocket. "We'll reroute. We can follow Free's tracks and still make it where we want to go if we pay attention. Follow me. We'll find her."

"Maybe…" She didn't want to voice her hope, and even more she didn't want to voice her fear. What if Free had found Dad and that was why she hadn't listened to Hilly's command?

What if Dad was—

She couldn't let her mind finish the thought. It was too ugly and scary and if she ignored the thought it didn't have to be real. That was what Dad always told her about her bad dreams.

"Follow me. We'll deal with what ifs once we find Free."

So, she did. She didn't have a lot of choices, really, but there was something about Cam's strong surety that made her believe she'd follow him even if she did have choices. He walked through the trees, following Free's tracks with an effortlessness that spoke of experience.

She could track a little. Dad did most of

the hunting, but she knew how. He'd taught her *some* of the skills to survive their clearing, if not the world.

Still, Cam was infinitely more capable. His strides were certain, his footfalls soft. He was a contradiction that way, always. Strong, steel-like facade. Kind, soft heart.

Every few yards he'd let out a sharp whistle, and instruct her to call out for Free. They wound farther and farther into the spindly, crowded pines. But the farther they climbed, the more the trees thinned out.

"If it gets too rocky we're going to lose her trail."

"We'll see," Cam replied, sounding wholly unworried. But the more they climbed, the more they were getting into the mountains. They'd be able to see farther, but they wouldn't be able to—

A sharp bark sounded through the trees.

"Free!"

More barking. Incessant. Cam took off in a jog toward the sound, so Hilly did, as well. Free met them on the trail, barking and turning in circles before she raced off again. This time, though, as they followed the agitated dog, she kept coming back, racing off, coming back. Barking the whole way.

Hilly was panting, but when she saw what

Free was leading them to, she forced herself to run even harder. She reached the horse tied to a tree and swallowed down the tears. "T.J.," Hilly breathed.

"Let me guess. Thomas Jefferson."

"I…" Hilly frowned as she rubbed her palm across the horse's neck. "Maybe. I don't know. I've only ever called him T.J."

"Your father's?"

Hilly nodded, scanning the area around the horse. There was no sign of her father or any of the gear he would have had with him. It looked like he'd stopped to give T.J. a rest but…

She focused on the horse as Cam looked around the area. She ran her hands over his mane, his flank, his legs. The horse barely moved, and though she wasn't a horse expert like Dad, his breathing seemed shallow. "He's been here awhile," Hilly noted, her stomach sinking as she found some feed in the saddle pack. "He's not in good shape at all."

Which hurt. Dad wouldn't have left T.J of his own volition. Ever.

Cam didn't respond as she put out the feed and searched for something to put some water in to give the horse a drink. Cam crouched next to her and rummaged around in his pack.

He pulled out a camping pot. It was small, but it would have to do. She filled it with water.

"We can't use him," Cam said, disappointment tinging the edges of his voice. "We'll have to call someone to come get him."

"Who's coming to do that?"

"Dylan can once the bank closes."

"He needs shelter now. Food and water." T.J. didn't touch the food or the water. He simply stood there.

Hilly swallowed at the emotion clogging her throat. The horse couldn't have been here the whole time Dad had been missing. He'd be dead of exposure at the very least. She didn't know if that was hope or not. Dad had been alive at least a few days ago.

But he'd left T.J. to basically die. That filled her with a hideous, heavy dread.

"We can't take him back to town. Your father was clearly here." Cam pointed to a set of footprints in the mud. They'd hardened over, so were easy to spot. "There are two sets of footprints here, Hilly. We need to follow that lead while we can."

He was right, of course. Rain or snow or even a hard wind could take out any trail they could find without warning. And Dad had been here sometime in the last forty-eight hours, she had to guess.

She looked at Cam helplessly. "Don't you know anyone else who could help him? We can't leave him."

Cam pulled a face and then sighed heavily. "Fine," he grumbled, pulling his phone out of his pocket. "But, boy, are you going to owe me."

# Chapter Nine

Cam grimaced with every punch of the button into his phone. He hated the fact he even knew this phone number. He hated the fact his brother was so dedicated to that damn bank he wouldn't take off to help Cam with a horse, a fact Cam didn't even question enough to consider calling Dylan.

But the only other person in his arsenal of people who would have the time, a horse trailer, the space and the inclination to help an ailing horse was the last person he wanted to call.

"Hello," a sweet, feminine voice answered with the sound of a kid yelling happily in the background.

"Hi, Addie. It's Cam."

"Oh, hi, Cam," Addie greeted, a thread of suspicion entering her voice. "Everything okay?"

He couldn't blame Addie for jumping to

things not being okay. Though Addie and Laurel were friends, and Addie sometimes joined in with family festivities since she was a distant Delaney relative, Cam didn't usually call up to her residence.

A *Carson* residence, because Addie had gone and married herself a Carson, despite that distant Delaney blood of hers.

"Everything is fine, but I…" He cleared his throat. "Is Noah around? I'd like to speak to him."

Addie was silent for so long he almost thought the phone had gone dead. "You… you want to talk to Noah."

"About a horse."

"You want to talk to Noah," she repeated.

"About a horse," he ground out through clenched teeth.

"All right," Addie said, clearly not feeling as though anything was all right. "Just a minute."

There was the muffled sound of voices, Addie's kid still yelling in the background, then a low male voice.

"What?"

"Carson," Cam greeted, trying not to sound like he felt. As though he was calling the devil. Silly overreaction, that. Maybe Delaneys had feuded with Carsons for over a century, but that was history and this was the present. This was for Hilly.

There was a long pause on Noah's end. "Yeah. What?"

"I need a favor."

A deep chuckle. "Oh, really? A favor for a Delaney."

Cam's jaw clenched. As much as he didn't believe in his father's obsession with the Carsons being bad blood, while the Delaneys were perfect—even more ludicrous now that Cam knew his father had had an affair with a *married* Carson—Cam did believe in the feud. He believed in history, and the way one family had flagrantly disobeyed rules and laws for over a century. It didn't mean all Delaneys were saints or all Carsons were evil, but it did mean he didn't trust a Carson as far as he could throw one.

Noah wasn't a bad guy, though. Not nearly as obnoxious as Grady Carson, Noah's cousin and Laurel's fiancé. Cam shouldn't be this reluctant to ask a Carson who had such ties to him for help, especially when Noah was one of the least obnoxious Carsons.

But Cam didn't want to do this. Because Noah, and likely all the Carsons, and possibly a few Delaneys, would hold this over his head for a while.

He glanced at Hilly, who was whispering soothing things to the horse. Free was pacing the area Cam had just searched. Worry permeated the air around them.

Cam closed his eyes and accepted his fate. Sometimes a man had to do uncomfortable, obnoxious things to help.

"I've found an abandoned horse in the woods north of town," Cam said, working carefully to make his tone devoid of any emotion. "It's been tied to a tree outside for I'd guess twenty-four to thirty-six hours and it's not in great shape. I've got a case I'm working for my security business and I'm in the middle of a lead, and Dylan's at work. Our ranch crew is on a drive."

"So I'm your last resort."

"Obviously." So much for diplomacy.

Noah chuckled a little at that, almost goodnaturedly. "I can probably come get it. You gonna pay for its upkeep till you can take it off my hands?"

"Of course."

"Delaneys," Noah muttered, as if Cam wasn't being more than generous.

"Where is this horse?"

Cam explained where they were.

"Gonna be tough getting a horse trailer up there."

"It is," Cam agreed. "And you'll have to do some hiking, but I can't let this lead go cold. And…" Cam scowled since Noah couldn't see him. "I need you not to tell Grady, because he'll only tell Laurel, and that's only going to get in the way of my case."

"Bending the law a bit, Delaney?" Noah asked, cheerful as Cam had ever heard him sound. He supposed sticking it to a Delaney was that enjoyable to him.

"Are you going to help?" Cam demanded irritably.

"Yeah, give me the directions again so I can write them down. We'll handle the horse till you can."

He relayed the directions once more, trying to be as specific as possible about the off-the-trail location of the horse. It galled him to have to say the next, but it was the right thing to do. "Thank you. We've got to get going, so the horse will be tied up and alone."

"We shouldn't be too long. I'll text you when the horse is safe."

"Good. Thanks." Cam clicked off the call and turned to see Hilly staring at him from where she stood, still gently petting the horse.

"You asked someone you hate to come get the horse."

"I don't hate Noah," Cam replied, uncomfortable that she'd picked up on all that. He didn't want to add worry onto her plate.

"You don't like him."

"It's complicated. And we have too much work to do to excavate how complicated." He went over to the set of footprints he'd found. "Two men. Can you tell from the print which one's your father?"

Hilly left her post by the horse and came to stand next to him. She stared down at the footprints, a line dug into her forehead. "I don't know. I'd guess the smaller one is my dad, but I don't know."

"As long as the footprints stay together, it doesn't matter," Cam said, more to himself. But if they diverged, things would get tricky. One step at a time. "Get your pack on."

"We can't leave him here," Hilly said, frowning at T.J.

"Help is on the way, Hilly. I promise. Noah's going to text me when they get him, so we'll know. I don't trust Carsons with a lot, but they'll take excellent care of a horse."

"You promise." She looked at the footprints on the ground, then the horse, then him. Her gaze was questioning, confused, but she straightened those shoulders and held his gaze. "You promise?" she demanded.

"I promise," he said, a solemn oath. It would

be such to anyone, because he didn't take his word lightly, but it somehow meant something more to say it to Hilly. He couldn't begin to count the things he'd sacrifice to keep his word to her.

"Okay," she said on an exhale. She pulled that determined aura around her as she held his gaze. "Okay, let's go find my father."

THE TRAIL WAS hard to follow. Too much rock, not enough mud to follow footprints easily. But Cam seemed to recognize things she didn't. A snapped tree branch, crushed grass. Hilly had no idea if they were on the right track, but Free following along without racing off again gave her hope.

They seemed to skirt the base of the impressive mountains, weaving this way and that through clearings or groves of aspen or pine. The air was cold, but the scenery took her breath away. When she got sight of the impressive peaks, they were craggy and white. When they passed by a pond or a creek, the water was always a clear, dazzling reflection of the vivid blue sky. She'd always loved the clearing she'd spent the past twenty years in. The way the sun warmed the pines in the summer, the way snow made everything blindingly white in the winter. It was home.

But this was the *world*.

Cam stopped, staring at a few rocks as if they were telling him secrets. Then he pulled out his map and his compass, and sat on a nearby fallen tree trunk. Though Dad had tried to teach her how to use a compass, she'd always been helplessly confused. Probably because she'd never been able to go very far away from the cabin—she hadn't needed to depend on a compass to bring her home.

"I think we're heading to the compound."

"Really?"

Cam nodded. He smoothed out his map. "We started here, then went in this direction to the horse." He tapped the spot they'd stopped. "We were somewhere in here. The compound is here. Following the trail your father and the other person left has led us straight west." He moved his long, capable fingers over the map, one finger reaching the other. Hilly watched those fingers, not sure what the tingling spreading along her skin meant.

She decided to ignore it.

A mechanical chirping sounded and Cam pulled out his phone. He scanned the screen, then shoved it back in his pocket. "Horse is safe and sound on the Carson ranch."

"Carson," she murmured. The name didn't

trigger quite as potent a sensation as when Laurel had said Hillary, but it was similar. An odd itchy feeling in her brain. Something recognizable but out of reach.

He looked up at her, eyebrow raised. "You know the Carsons?"

"No, I just…"

Cam stood, putting the map and compass back in his pocket while he studied her. "Just what?" he demanded.

"I don't know. I don't."

She saw the flicker of unease in his expression, a second of distrust, before he smoothed it away until his face offered nothing at all.

It made her desperate to explain herself. Even as her mind admonished her not to trust him with everything, to be careful and keep some things to herself. The words tumbled out as if to escape her inner admonitions. "It's a feeling I can't explain. Like when Laurel said Hillary. Or when I saw the picture of the eagle—only, that I could recognize. These names I can't, but they give me a *feeling*. I know that doesn't make any sense, but—"

"It doesn't have to. Some things don't. Gut feelings. Maybe old memories. I just want you to tell me when you get that feeling, okay? Maybe eventually it helps us piece something together."

"But they could be wrong. Silly, pointless—"

Cam shook his head, striding along whatever path he had in his mind. "It doesn't matter. Better to sift through everything than miss something because we think it's silly."

There was that word again. *We*. He kept including her, like they were a team. It was a sharp contrast to how her father had always treated her. Which she supposed could be normal. Dad called the shots and she was expected to follow. Maybe all father-daughter relationships were like that, and maybe other relationships were more like this. A partnership where people brought two equal things to the table.

She bit her lip against the inappropriate smile that threatened her mouth. She was scared sick over her father's disappearance, over T.J. being abandoned, but there was something amazing about having someone to share her worry with, her determination to find Dad with. It made her feel stronger, not weaker.

Cam stopped in a small clearing. They'd traversed up and down different altitudes all afternoon. They were somewhere in the middle right now. Not down in the muddy earth, but not up in the craggy mountains. The ground under their feet was smooth rock, but boulders surrounded the space to create a kind of alcove.

"We'll camp here tonight."

"Shouldn't we keep going?"

"We don't want to get turned around in the dark. And we can't show up at the compound at a weird time. They have to believe we're a couple trying to find asylum with the Protectors, not two people rushing to find someone who might be in trouble."

It was smart, of course, but Dad wouldn't have left T.J. of his own volition. Even if Cam said there was no sign of a scuffle or altercation, and that it looked as if Dad had gone along easily enough, Hilly knew what he wasn't saying. Hilly knew there would have to be a reason Dad left the horse.

Probably a gun, or some kind of weapon, that threatened him to come along with the other person and leave the horse behind.

In Hilly's mind, there was no other possible answer to Dad leaving T.J.

So, her father was being led around by another man, likely with a weapon, and Cam expected her to camp and wait.

"Hilly." Cam stood in front of her. In a

slow move that had her holding her breath, he reached out and undid the backpack's snap over her chest. She was wearing three layers, including an oversized heavy coat, and could barely feel the brush of his hands as he undid the clasp at her waist, as well. Still, her body felt as though it was going haywire—nerves misfiring and skin overheating.

The strangest part was it wasn't *unpleasant*. She wanted to explore that jittering thing inside of her, and see how far it would go.

"I know you're worried about your father's safety, but let's consider this. If he was coerced away from the horse by force, that means whoever did so wanted to keep him alive. He's being taken somewhere, likely to the compound. And, yes, I won't lie, he may be in danger, but it's not fatal danger or that would have already happened."

Icy cold diluted all that intriguing heat. "It doesn't mean it couldn't happen at the compound. That they're bringing him there to do something awful—"

He gently pulled the pack off her shoulders, then went through the mesmerizing moves of taking off his own. "Thinking about the worst-case scenarios doesn't solve anything, and it puts us in danger. We have to be methodical. I know he's your father, and your emotional responses are valid, but trust my method to keep him and us as safe as we can be."

"I'm doing nothing but trusting you."

"I know." He smiled ruefully. "Don't think I take that lightly, Hilly, because I don't." He pulled some things off his pack with deft, certain movements.

"I don't know anything about setting up camp," Hilly murmured, feeling unaccountably useless all of a sudden.

"That's all right. One tent won't take much time." He looked around the sky as he knelt to unload more supplies. "I brought MREs so we won't need a fire."

*One tent.* She was going to sleep in the same tent as him?

He grinned up at her. "Sorry, military talk. MREs are ready-to-eat meals. Well, meals, ready to eat. I figured that'd be easier than trying to cook," he explained, as if that was the reason for the shocked expression on her face, not knowing what his acronym stood for.

But she didn't care about that. They were going to sleep in the *same* tent. Her insides jumped with nerves. She couldn't even explain why. Cam wasn't going to do anything to her.

He worked silently on putting up the tent, and Hilly just stood there feeling useless, extraneous and like her face was on fire.

"Why don't you get Free some water?" Cam suggested gently as the tent took shape.

"Right. Sure." Water the dog. Sit here and stare at the teeny, tiny tent she was going to share with a *man*, and worry that her father had been forcibly kidnapped by some strange antigovernment group he may or may not belong to that she and Cam were going to pretend to want to join.

No big deal. Not at all.

## Chapter Ten

"We should try to get some sleep," Cam said as the riotous color of sunset began to fade into nothing but darkness and starlight. "We should be able to reach the compound tomorrow if we're well rested."

He couldn't see Hilly's expression, only the shadow of her body perched on a rock, Free's shadow curled up on the ground next to her.

She didn't say anything or make a move. She was pensive, edgy. Clearly, she was worried about her father, and she should be. Something wasn't right here.

He wished there was some way to set her mind at ease, but the best he'd been able to give her was the knowledge that if they wanted her father dead, he'd already *be* dead. But that didn't mean things couldn't have gone down at the compound. *If* that was even how this all connected.

Cam got up from the rock he'd been sitting

on. He'd already packed out the trash and the food and hung it from a tree away from the tent to keep the potential threat of bears from the campsite.

The tent was set up and he had to admit the prospect of them sharing it was…uncomfortable. As much as he was used to not having space of his own, not having much of anything of his *own* after over a decade in the Marines, he wasn't used to sharing space with, well, a woman. At least not a woman he wasn't blood related to, and the women he was related to weren't vulnerable, overly sheltered enigmas.

"What if Free wanders off?" Hilly asked, a slight tremor in her voice.

"We can see if we can fit her into the tent."

Hilly looked at the small space dubiously, but she didn't voice any objections.

He forced himself to smile as if this was the most casual, normal thing on the planet. He gestured to the tent flap. "Ladies first."

Again she looked dubiously at the tent, but this time she made a move for it. She unzipped the flap and crawled inside. Free sniffed at the opening and then followed Hilly in.

Cam glanced around the clearing, then up at the starry sky before he followed. He was half tempted to sleep out here. It wouldn't be the first time he'd slept under the stars instead of inside a tent.

But it was a two-person tent. And he was an adult who could handle this task he'd taken on. The most important thing was keeping Hilly safe while they tried to figure out what had happened to her father and who burned down her cabin and why.

Some uncomfortable interpersonal awkwardness was hardly important in the face of a mission.

With great force of will, he crouched down and crawled into the tent.

Hilly was huddled in a corner, the weak battery-powered lantern making her half shadow, half woman. She stared with great concern at the two rolled-up sleeping bags he'd tossed inside earlier. Free had happily stretched herself out across the middle of the tent floor, making the space look even smaller.

Hilly cleared her throat as Cam focused on zipping the flap closed.

"I wasn't sure how to…position the sleeping bags," she offered.

Cam turned. "Free's not giving us much space."

But Hilly didn't smile or chuckle. She just kept looking very, very concerned.

Which was understandable, he had to remind himself. He was mostly a stranger to her, and she had a lot to worry about. He couldn't take away her concern or nerves, but maybe by acting like he didn't have any he'd be able to put her at *some* ease.

He grabbed the first sleeping bag and rolled it out on one side of Free. Then rolled out the other in the space next to the door. It'd be tight, but he'd nudge the dog over if he had to.

Hilly moved slowly and with some trepidation, but she wiggled herself down into the bag, facing him. Her dark, worried gaze forced him to act as though everything was normal.

He unclasped the gun holster from his pants, then carefully set both in the corner of the tent closest to his head. He could feel Hilly's eyes on him while he did it, but she didn't say anything. So, he slid into the bag himself, then when Hilly held up the lantern with a raised eyebrow, he nodded. She switched it off, and everything went black.

He could smell the plastic of the tent, the pungent scent of dog, a wisp of that fresh, clean night air that had come in with them.

And he could smell her. Shampoo, he supposed. Something fruity that had come from his sister's bathroom and was now lodged in her hair. Her skin.

He stared hard at the night, making out the lines of the tent as his eyes adjusted to the dark. He listened and the tent filled with noises of dog breathing, human breathing, the slide of sleeping bag against tent floor as Hilly fidgeted.

He didn't. He lay perfectly still, fighting the whispers in the dark. The memories. The guilt that had made him afraid to sleep those first few months home.

But he'd settled into home, into civilian life. It was just being out here, having a mission, so to speak, that reminded him of his old life, and his old life had all sorts of sharp wounds that hadn't so much healed as scarred over.

"Cam?"

He breathed out, focusing on her voice. Hilly had nothing to do with his military life or his failures. There was some comfort in that.

"Yeah?"

"Do you really think this group is just going to believe our story? We're going to waltz in and they're going to…let us?"

"No."

He heard her move, like she'd shot straight

up into a sitting position. "What?" she demanded with a bit of a screech.

"They're isolated and wary of outsiders. They're on government watch lists. No, they're not going to trust us right off the bat. I'm sure there will be some kind of test or something."

"Test?" she said with increasing alarm.

"We don't need to worry about that."

"A dangerous, isolated group giving us tests. Sure. No worries here," she grumbled.

Cam smiled into the dark. "They're going to be suspicious of our motives, but we don't have to worry because they're going to assume we're FBI or ATF or some kind of government organization. They're not going to be looking for civilians on the hunt for a missing man. Whatever tests we get, we'll pass. We're not who they're protecting themselves against."

"If my dad is there, won't they suspect someone is looking for him?"

"It's a long shot."

"But it's possible."

"Anything's possible, Hilly. We have to play the odds."

She made a sound, something like a huff.

"Get some sleep. We've still got a ways to hike tomorrow."

Cam settled into the dark and quiet. Let himself get used to the shuffle of brush in the wind. He yawned as Free made a quiet huffing noise. His body relaxed, his eyes closed…

The faint crack of a twig jerked him fully awake from his almost doze. He might have convinced himself he was half dreaming if a growl hadn't started low in Free's throat. He could feel the rumble of that growl pressed up next to him.

"Easy," he whispered to the dog, straining to listen to what might be outside the tent. It could be anything. The wind. An animal. Human.

"Cam," Hilly whispered. "I heard—"

He reached across the dog between them and found her arm and gave it a squeeze signaling her to be quiet.

The most likely explanation was an animal, but the hairs on the back of his neck were raised and something lodged deep in his gut pinged with an intuition he'd learned to trust in similar situations.

Some small part of his brain reminded him he wasn't deployed anymore. This wasn't war. But something about that noise didn't sit right.

He reached for the gun and carefully and quietly slid it out of its holster. "Stay," he commanded in a whisper, both to Hilly and the dog.

She didn't argue, though he suspected she wanted to. Keeping his breathing steady, he pulled the zipper of the door down, millimeter by millimeter, trying to minimize the amount of noise he made.

Once he unzipped the flap enough to slide out, he paused, listening intently to the world around them.

Hilly was silent. She might even be holding her breath, and Free seemed to sense the situation enough to stay still, as well.

Cam slid out into the darkness. The moon and stars shone bright enough to give the world around him something of a glow, but it was still dark. He listened carefully, trying to discern the difference between scurrying animals or the wind, and something that might be human.

He stood and listened and listened and listened. Nothing moved. Nothing seemed out of place. Even that gut feeling eased. Still, he waited. When he got to the edge of his patience, he forced himself to wait more. To analyze every swish, thwack and creak.

But in the end, there was nothing. If someone had been out there, they were gone. It was nearly worse than an assault, just the potential someone was out there. Watching them. Following them. Knowing things Cam didn't know.

Frustrated but satisfied they were once again alone, he crept back into the tent. "Nothing," he muttered to Hilly.

"Are you sure?"

Cam sighed. "No. Which is why I'm going to stay up. You go to sleep."

"How could I possibly sleep?"

"By trying. I'll listen and watch out while you catch a few hours, and then we'll switch." He didn't have plans to actually switch, but he knew he'd get less argument from her if he claimed he was going to. Maybe it had been a while, but he was used to long days and sleepless nights. It was more important for Hilly to get rest.

"Cam."

"It was probably nothing. This is all a precaution." Of course, he didn't believe that either. But what was more important? Hilly trusting him or Hilly relaxing enough to catch a few hours of sleep?

"Yeah, right," she muttered, but she scooted down in the sleeping bag. She tossed and turned for a few minutes. But when she stilled, she spoke instead of slept.

"I know you're trying to protect me, or

something like that. I think that's what my father was trying to do, too. I don't know why he went missing, or how exactly he was involved with this group, but I think he knew that whatever connection he had to them put me in danger. But look what happened to him. He's missing and probably hurt. I don't need to be protected. Protecting me left me in danger and in the dark, and I won't let anyone do that to me again."

Hilly could have no idea the way those words pierced him, and uncovered every insecurity he had about where he'd gone wrong with Aaron—thinking he had it handled, thinking if he was vigilant and careful, Aaron would be okay. But he hadn't been.

Cam focused on his breathing as the emotional pain swept through, searing and total.

When he trusted his voice, he spoke the truth. "I'll wake you up in three hours."

Hilly hadn't thought she'd sleep. She was too worried, too afraid and too frustrated with how little she understood about everything. But the next thing she knew she was being nudged awake, Cam's low voice in her ear.

"Your turn, if you want to take it."

She struggled to push away the fog of sleep and concentrate on the here and now.

Well, not too much of the *here* because Cam was crouched over her in the dark, and there was something altogether unalarming about the large shadow looming above her. Because Cam didn't scare her, even though she knew he should.

But he'd kept his promise. It was still dark and he was waking her up to take her turn as watch. That meant something.

She rubbed her hands over her face in an effort to wipe away all the sleep cobwebs that were clouding her focus. She sat up and Free whimpered. "I think Free needs to go out."

"I'll go with you. We don't want to be wandering off alone, even with Free."

She considered arguing. After all she'd lived in her little cabin in the woods for days at a time all by herself. She could handle taking Free outside.

Except back then she'd had a cabin as shelter and a belief she was safe. She did not feel safe here. She felt targeted, and the only reason it didn't steal over her like panic was because of Cam. Somehow, this strange man was her anchor in chaos.

He unzipped the flap and stepped into the cold night. Hilly shivered against it, though she'd never taken off her coat. It was amazing how much warmth had packed into the tent, and how frigid the air felt out here.

"Do your business, Free," she urged.

The dog ambled off, sniffing the ground as she went, and she and Cam followed—her holding the camping lantern and Cam holding a more high-powered flashlight.

"Why didn't you use the flashlight earlier?" she asked, as he swept the bright beam over the ground, rocks, trees. She kept an eye on Free's shadow.

"If someone was out here, I didn't want them to have a clear glimpse of me. They had too much of an advantage in their position for it to work out well for me."

She wished that *if* gave her more comfort, but it didn't. She knew what she'd heard. A snap, and while it could have been animal in nature, that would have been one big animal.

Cam kept moving his beam of light around the clearing, and Hilly followed him even as she kept an eye on Free. Truth be told, she didn't want to be more than arm's reach away from Cam until morning.

"Footprint," Cam said, somewhat disgustedly, his flashlight pointing to a spot between two rocks.

"Dad's?" she asked hopefully.

"I don't think so. It's not a clear print—

someone tried to hide it. But you can get an idea of the outline." He nodded her toward the beam of light, so she took a few steps closer.

Smooshed in between two rocks was a small oval of mud. She peered down at the mark, seeing maybe a disturbance in the ground, but not really an outline. She glanced up at Cam. She could only make out his profile in the glow of the flashlight. He wasn't saying it, but she could tell he didn't like this simply from the tenseness in his jaw.

Hilly looked out into the inky dark, trying not to panic at the idea that someone was out there lurking and hiding their footprints.

Cam patted his leg quietly. "Come on, Free," he said on a near whisper as his hand closed over her arm. He pulled her back to the tent, nudging Hilly and then Free inside before he followed.

"What would someone have been doing just walking around out there?" Hilly asked, rubbing her hands over her arms and trying to feel warm again. Steady.

"Likely just determining who we are," Cam said flatly. "How many. Maybe trying to get an idea of our purpose. Information gathering."

"But *who* is information gathering on us?"

"Don't know," Cam said, turning off his flashlight.

"I don't like that answer."

He chuckled a little bit as he fit his large body into his sleeping bag. She sat cross-legged on hers, keeping the lantern switched on.

"Like it or not," he said in between a yawn, "it's the truth. It could be anyone."

Anyone. What an awful, awful thought.

He tossed his phone to her. "I set the timer. When it goes off, just hit the stop button that pops up. Then we'll pack up and get hiking." He settled into his sleeping bag. "Any suspicious sounds and you wake me up. You need to talk? Wake me up. Free needs out or—"

"I get it. If there's a problem, wake you up."

He shifted back and forth in the sleeping bag, and she shouldn't watch him. There was something private about a man settling into a tiny, lifeless camping pillow and closing his eyes. Private or not, Hilly was captivated.

He was a big man, and the quick sleep he'd fallen into and the heavy sleeping bag encasing his large body did nothing to lessen the impact of that. He dwarfed Free and made Hilly feel small when usually she was the tallest person in the room.

She turned off the light and closed her eyes. Hardly the point of her life right now. The point was she was supposed to be listening for anything suspicious. Gritty-eyed and with a nervy exhaustion dogging her, Hilly played every mental game she could think of, but her mind kept wandering to where her father was.

Was he okay? Was he even alive?

She swallowed against the wave of fear. He'd be the first to chastise her to be practical. To think of the here and now. You couldn't change the past. You could only work toward the future.

Her future would include solving this mystery. One way or another.

So she told herself, over and over again, in an endless cycle of worry, panic, then reassurance leading to determination.

She wasn't certain how much time had passed when Cam started to move. Not get up or out of his sleeping bag, but a tossing and turning she wouldn't have expected from him. He was usually so still.

When his moving became something more like thrashing, Hilly's heart stuttered a beat. He mumbled something, and though she couldn't make out the words she could *feel* the distress waving off of him.

Frozen between letting him work through it on his own, and this awful, compelling need to make it stop for him, the thrashing got worse, the murmurs turning more desperate. To the point she couldn't take it.

Free whimpered, nudging Cam's form under the sleeping bag with her nose, so Hilly moved next to her, doing the same—only with her hand instead of her nose. She nudged his arm.

"Cam," she whispered, not sure what awaited her when he woke up, but determining to be brave enough to handle it. "Cam," she said louder.

His eyes flew open, and his entire body went on alert as if ready for an attack. He looked around without moving, though his muscles were tense and ready to strike. She could see him come back to himself, understand where he was, slowly let the muscles relax.

"You were having a bad dream."

"Is that what that was?" he replied blandly.

She read the warning tone in his voice. She knew enough about those. Her father had plenty of places she wasn't allowed to go. It would only take that cool, flat voice to make her retreat.

And look where she'd ended up. Homeless and alone. She'd be utterly helpless and powerless without Cam's help. She wouldn't let anyone, even Cam, put her back in a place where she didn't know the puzzle pieces of her own life.

Right now, like it or not on either of their sides, Cam was a piece of her life. So, she'd push. Ask. Demand answers. It didn't have to be *fair* or *right*, since he was a stranger. She needed more than a stranger or even more than a protector on her side. She needed an equal.

"Is it because of what you told me about the man in your unit?"

There was silence, not even the sound of a breath taken or exhaled. He didn't move a *muscle*, so neither did she.

Finally, he sighed. "Sometimes."

"What is it other times?" she asked, unable to help herself. She wanted to understand how someone so strong and sure when he was awake could fall into something so... He'd seemed helpless. Oh, he'd snapped out of it in a second, but for a moment he'd seemed lost.

"War, Hilly. Not a picnic."

Right. War. He was a soldier. He'd seen things. She'd studied enough wars and conflicts through her father's rigid history teachings that she understood what soldiers saw, and how it might haunt them.

What she'd never understood, no matter how her father had praised courage and bravery in fighting to protect, was *why*. Why did some people get to do that and some people were hidden away in cabins protected from an outside world for their whole lives?

"Why do you think you should be the one to help? I mean, what makes you feel like out of all the people in the world you should risk yourself for someone else?"

"Because I can or could. Because it's the right thing to do. Then. Now. Maybe that sounds oversimplistic, but it's the core of who I am. I don't know how to explain it any differently than that."

"I think I understand," she said quietly. Maybe not fully, but in that moment of watching him struggle with the dream, she'd wanted to help. Not because she should, but because someone should and she was here.

She wanted to find her father, even if it meant trusting Cam and infiltrating this dangerous group, because she loved her father and she didn't want anything bad to happen to him.

She stared at Cam, and though she could only make out the murky shadow of him, she *felt* as though he were staring back. Studying her. Assessing her, but not in a bad way, exactly. She didn't understand it, or the way her breath bunched up in her lungs.

When a mechanical sound trilled through the air, she jumped a foot.

"My alarm," he said, his voice still flat. He reached over to grab the phone and made the noise stop with a push of his finger against the screen. "Time to pack up. We've got some hiking ahead of us."

"Cam…" But he just kept moving, rolling up his sleeping bag, expressly not looking at her.

She wanted to protect. Like he'd done when he'd helped her out of the cabin, when he'd made her stay in the tent to see what the noise was. She wanted to be brave, and step between him and danger, between her father and danger.

For the first time in her life, she had the chance to be the one fighting for the right side of things, instead of hidden in the cabin.

She was going to take it.

## Chapter Eleven

The morning was cold, and Cam wished he'd taken the time to heat up water for coffee. He missed his bed and the ranch work that steadied him the morning after a dream. He missed his routine, and for the first time since he'd seen Hilly in the police station, he wished he hadn't.

He couldn't seem to lie to her. He didn't care for her earnestness or her complete lack of reading a situation enough to know not to ask an uncomfortable question.

Not her fault, but that didn't put him at ease. He was only glad they were approaching where the compound should be, and he could focus on that.

"Do you want to go over it one more time?" he asked, studying the rocky outcroppings and tree line as he adjusted his backpack on his shoulders.

He heard her inhale and exhale. "You're

Cameron Tyler. I'm Leigh Tyler. Married a year ago." She went through the details of their fake courtship and marriage that they'd lined out together. "We're just looking for a life of freedom."

"It's not just about freedom. It's about shrugging off the bonds of tyranny."

"Now, that *does* sound like my dad."

"They'll expect you to talk a certain way. Now, we're playing roles here, so I'm going to do most of the talking. You won't like everything I say, but you're going to smile and nod and pretend like you agree wholeheartedly no matter what."

"What *kinds* of things are you planning on saying?"

"It's not that I'm planning on saying anything in particular. It's just they'll expect me to be in charge, and you to be…" He knew how his sisters would react if he explained any of this to them. Trying to inflict great bodily harm on him regardless of how little he agreed with it.

"What?" Hilly demanded.

Cam glanced back at her. She really was clueless. "Let's just say these kind of guys see a woman as… They expect people in a relationship to have certain roles. My role will be a more leadership one. Your role will be more…domestic."

"Ah. I cook. I clean. I'm in the dark about every important decision. Yes, believe it or not, I'm familiar with that one. Though to be fair I didn't care so much about a woman's place being in the home until I was left helpless in the home."

He wanted to glance back at her again, get a read on her expression. Those words were bitter to an extent, but with a certain amount of acceptance. But the rocks were loose here and the trail steep, so he kept his eyes on the ground. "Just don't take anything I say to heart, okay? It's not my opinions or thoughts. Everything I say is all for the end result."

"I'm not sure I'll be good at acting. Being *Leigh Tyler* and shrugging off the bonds of anything, let alone tyranny."

"Don't consider it acting. I'm going to be doing the acting. You're the observer. You watch people. Pay attention to what they say, how they act, where they go. Their suspicion will focus more on me than you, so you'll have more opportunity to pay attention without them noticing anyway."

"And what if my dad isn't there?"

"If that's the case, then we'll say we miss the convenience of life on the grid and want to head home. Or we'll sneak away and find a new lead."

"You think we'll have to *sneak* away?"

He shrugged, trying to sound unconcerned. "Probably not. It's not a cult. Exactly."

"Wow. That's reassuring," she muttered.

Cam wanted to find the right words to set her at ease, but he felt a prickle at the back of his neck. "Someone's close," he said as quietly as he could. "Just keep following me."

Hilly stumbled a bit, and Cam tried not to scowl. She was right. She was not going to be good at the acting thing, but it wasn't fair to expect her to be.

She caught herself before she fell and they hiked on, toward where he'd figured out the compound might be.

Whoever was out there followed, and Cam figured if this was a test, it wouldn't do to act like a total moron. A lot of the Protectors were former military, according to what he'd read about the group, and he planned to use his own service to suit that purpose. Which meant he had to at least act like a Marine.

So, on occasion, he'd stop Hilly and pretend to study the woods. Sometimes he'd point in the direction he thought they might be, and whisper something encouraging to

Hilly about how good they were doing if someone was following them.

She didn't seem to share his happiness over that fact, but it wasn't the be-all and end-all. It'd be easy to convince whoever needed convincing he was all in, and his wife had her reservations, without that looking poorly on his chances with the group.

He had to hope.

He wasn't startled when a man melted into view seemingly out of nowhere, planting himself in the path Cam had been following. Cam had felt his approach in a way he couldn't explain exactly, but he still tried to school his face to look surprised. A flicker of unease, and then the careful banking of it as he would have done if these were his Marine days and someone had come out of nowhere at him.

He stopped in the trail, positioning himself in front of Hilly. A spousal protective instinct this man could hopefully appreciate. "It's okay, honey," he said, in a low, soothing voice. He kept his gaze on the man in their way. "Are you a Protector?" he asked.

The man was tall and broad shouldered, but more lean than burly. He wore fatigue pants and a brown Henley. A dark beard covered his face and he wore a camo hat pulled low so Cam couldn't get a good read on him. He had a gun strapped to his chest, and if Cam's instincts were still on point, a lot more weapons were on him. Hidden.

The man gave no answer to Cam's question, and didn't move. He stood still as a statue blocking Cam and Hilly's forward progress.

"We wanted to join," Cam continued. "If you are one of the Protectors. That's what we're looking for. I've been reading a lot about you guys." He worked on sounding eager, and in the end it wasn't hard because he was eager. To get to the bottom of this and give Hilly the answers she deserved.

"Can't believe everything you read on the internet," the man said gruffly.

"No, sir. You sure can't, but I figured it was worth a shot to find out for myself." He stood a little straighter, as if the opinion of a strange man with assessing eyes mattered to him.

"You in trouble?"

Cam adopted a somewhat sheepish expression. "A little. Nothing major. I'm not running from anything. Had a small wheat operation, but all these government agencies are squeezing me out of business with a bunch of overreaching regulations. I got into it with some bureaucrat and I'm over it. Something needs to be done."

The man studied him, and though Cam knew how to read an enemy, this man was a blank slate. It caused a sliver of unease to press down on his chest, but he didn't let that show.

"Follow me," the man said, abruptly turning and beginning to stalk the same way Cam had been headed.

He glanced back at Hilly, trying to communicate with a look this was good. Surely the man had bought Cam's story and was leading them to the compound. Maybe there'd be a test or two first, or an attempt to disorient them, but this was the first step he'd wanted.

Hilly didn't look at all assured or happy, but he couldn't let that stop him from hurrying after the man, Hilly and Free following after.

*Yours to keep safe.*

*We know how well that went last time.*

Cam shoved the old voice out of his head and focused on the mission instead.

THE PACE WAS PUNISHING. Sometimes Hilly had to jog to keep up. They seemed to walk in circles, up mountains and down, and yet the terrain all looked the same and she couldn't help but wonder if this man was just trying to walk them to the point of delirium.

If Cam had any similar reservations, they didn't show. She had to admit it was impressive how he'd sounded when he'd talked to the man. Like someone else.

Impressive, but also scary. Which one was the real Cam? Much as she figured it was the one she knew, the fact he could put on such a convincing mask, and so easily...

Well, it didn't matter as long as he led her to her father. End of story.

"My wife's getting a little tired," Cam said to the man leading them.

Hilly was surprised, both at the odd jolt the word *wife* gave her, and at the fact Cam had noticed how hard she was struggling when he hadn't looked back at her once.

"Sounds like a you problem." But the man stopped, pulling a water bottle out of his pack.

Cam did the same, but instead of taking a drink, he handed it to her. Hilly took it and sipped, hoping the longer she took to drink, the longer they could rest. God, she wished she could sit down, but the man was staring at her.

Hilly shifted and looked away, but she could *feel* his gaze still on her. There was an intensity to his stare that made shaky nerves work through her body. She didn't feel threatened, so to speak. She felt seen through. Like he could read every last fact about her with that long, intimidating glare.

"We're almost there," he said after a while.

When Hilly dared glance at him again, he was filling a small plastic bowl with water. He whistled Free over, and the dog happily trotted to him and began to drink the water. It was a nice gesture, but that only made her more nervous.

She glanced at Cam. For the first time, the eager mask he'd been wearing the whole time had fallen, and he looked grim and suspicious. In his hands he held his own bowl for Free, though he hadn't filled it.

"You've got a good dog here," the man said, running a hand over Free's head. He glanced up and locked eyes with Hilly.

Again, it wasn't threatening in a way that made sense to Hilly, but she wished she'd left Free with the Delaneys. Wished she'd done so many things differently, because the man kept looking at *her*, not Cam. Something wasn't right about that, considering even with Cam's act, it was pretty clear he'd be more of a threat to the man than Hilly.

"She's the best," Cam said proudly, his mask back in place.

"Quiet one you got here," the man said, nodding to Hilly, and his brown eyes never left her face. "What did you say your name was again?"

Cam opened his mouth, but the man held up a hand. "I'm asking her."

"We didn't tell you our names," Hilly replied, not missing the way Cam closed his eyes as if disappointed in her answer. He wanted her to *act*, but she didn't know how.

The man nodded thoughtfully, scratching Free behind the ears. It was a friendly touch and yet it took everything Hilly had not to call Free back to her, not to jerk her away from this dangerous man.

"What's your name then?" he asked.

"Leigh."

"Leigh what?"

"Leigh Tyler."

"And do you want to be here, Leigh Tyler?"

Panic had her whipping her head to Cam. What was the man getting at?

"I didn't ask your husband, ma'am. I asked you. Do you want to be here?"

Hilly swallowed, trying to remember everything Cam had told her. Be as truthful as possible. The closer to the truth they kept, the harder it would be for them to catch her in a lie.

So much for Cam doing all the talking. "I'm on the fence."

The man raised an eyebrow. "You're on the fence, but you're here."

"It means a lot to Cameron," she said, glancing at Cam helplessly. She couldn't read his expression. Couldn't be sure she was doing the right thing at all. She thought about what Cam had said regarding the group's thoughts on men and women, and decided to be like Cam. Play her role. "I trust Cameron's decision making. That's why I'm here."

The man considered this. He gave Free one last pet, then picked up the bowl Free had emptied and shoved both it and the water bottle into his pack. Then, without a word, he began to walk again.

Free trotted happily after him, then Cam, then her. Her feet screamed in pain and exhaustion, but there was no choice but to hike after them.

Behind his back, Cam gave her a thumbs-up, which made her relax a little. She'd done the right thing. Cam approved. She could breathe again.

At least until the man led them into a small clearing. There was a large tent on one side, more of a lean-to with canvas covering all but one side. There were a few people inside who appeared to be cooking over a fire pit or washing dishes in a tub of water.

On the other side of the clearing was a handful of small tents, all the same canvas color and uniform distances apart. They weren't like the backpacking tent Cam had brought, but more of a square shape, taller, like you could stand up inside them. Everything was oppressively quiet.

It gave Hilly the creeps. But they were here. Was her father? Could this all be over? God, she hoped so.

The man leading them kept walking, straight to a tent in the middle of the line. He pointed at the flap. "This will be yours. Put your things inside, then come to the common area." He pointed to the lean-to. "I'll have a lunch prepared for you."

"I've got food. We don't need—"

"You'll do as I say, thank you," the man said, and then was striding away toward the lean-to.

Cam shrugged and lifted the flap, stepping inside. Free followed, so Hilly did, as well. Inside wasn't tent-like either. There was a small cot in one corner, an empty basin in another. The ground beneath their feet was mostly dirt, as though all the grass had been trampled away.

Was her father in one of those other tents? Were they safe here? Too many questions were lodged in her chest and made it hard to breathe. Cam didn't say anything, and that made the pressure worse.

He set his backpack down by the basin, and gestured her to do the same without a word. She did while he looked around, examining the canvas walls, the ground, before he came back to stand next to her. He leaned close, so close, she could only stand frozen as he whispered into her ear.

"This isn't it."

"What do you mean?" she asked, full volume, wincing at the sound of her own voice echoing through the tent.

Cam shook his head, then rested his hands on her shoulders, keeping her close so he could whisper in her ear again.

"Don't know who's listening, so whisper. This isn't the compound. It's a test. This place is some kind of decoy. But I'm betting if we convince them we're the people we say we are, they'll move us to the main one."

It was strange to have words leave a cold ball of fear in her stomach, while the brush of his breath against her ear made her skin feel hot.

"How long?" she asked, remembering to whisper this time. She didn't lean forward to his ear, though. They stood practically nose to nose, his hands still on her shoulders, a heavy, strong weight. Like an anchor.

His expression went to that focused intensity of following a mission to something softer, something like regret. This close she could see the makeup of the hazel in his eyes, the play of brown and green. She could see the growth of whiskers across his jaw, little prickles of darkness against the fair hue of his skin. His mouth looked soft this close.

She blinked, not sure what avenues her brain was trying to go down. It made her achy, and it made her want to lean into him.

Which was insanity.

He leaned forward again, his mouth against her ear. She shivered involuntarily, wondering if he would read into what he could surely feel under his palms. The unsteadiness in her. The kind that had nothing to do with the situation they were in.

But when he spoke in that intimate whisper, he was all business. "Have to take it day by day, all right? We just do what he says, and we pay attention."

She wanted to close her eyes and cry. Maybe crawl onto the cot and sleep for a day so her legs would stop throbbing with pain.

Cam pulled away from her, but he lifted his palm to her cheek, gentle and somehow soothing in the midst of all this turmoil. He held her gaze.

"It's going to be okay," he said firmly, in full voice, completely and utterly sure of himself.

Her stomach flipped. Not just at the words, but at the rough palm on her cheek. That his hand could be that big, that rough, and gentle at the same time, sent another shudder through her, but his words steadied her.

Hilly hadn't made a lot of decisions in her life, but the past few days had been all about them. All about Cam allowing her some of her own decisions.

So, right here, right now, she decided to believe him.

## Chapter Twelve

Cam led Hilly back outside the tent-like structure. The afternoon had grown warm, and the sun was shining. This small compound was eerily quiet, and he'd only seen four people so far.

It had to be a decoy compound of some sort. There were only women and the man who'd led them here. Unless the men were purposefully out of sight.

It was possible. He didn't *feel* watched, but he wouldn't let that put him at ease.

He glanced back at Hilly. She definitely wasn't at ease, but he liked to think he'd comforted her some. She looked worried, but not quite so panicked as she had been when they'd arrived in the clearing.

"Have a seat," one of the women said as Cam approached. "We've been told you've had a long journey. You must be hungry."

Her voice was warm, the words kind, but

Cam couldn't shake the creepy feeling wiggling up his spine. Still, he took a seat at the picnic table she'd gestured to and motioned for Hilly to sit next to him.

"What a sweet dog," the woman said in the same pleasant tone. "Gayle, why don't you find her some scraps? You don't mind, do you?" the woman asked of them.

"No. Go right ahead. Thank you for thinking of her," Cam answered.

She smiled at them. "Aren't you two so sweet?" She sighed, almost dreamily. "You'll be cured of that soon enough," she said just as cheerfully before heading over to where another woman stood next to a stack of dishes.

Cam forced himself not to stare at her, reminded himself it didn't matter if she meant that as a general view on the eventuality of relationships souring or if it was some kind of warning or *what*.

But that flutter of concern was out of place, because Hilly and he weren't in any relationship, and they were only in this place to find her father. There was nothing to be "cured of" regardless of what the woman had said.

There were two women in the lean-to, though there had been three before when they'd arrived. The man who'd led them here was nowhere to be seen.

A bowl of some kind of stew was placed in front of him and one in front of Hilly. It was followed by a tin cup of milk, and a bread roll on a paper towel.

It was all so kind and accommodating, Cam wondered for a moment if it was poisoned. He glanced at the woman who'd brought them the food, but she'd already bustled back to the fire and wasn't paying him any mind.

He glanced at Hilly, who was looking down at the bowl with the same concern on her face.

But they didn't have much of a choice if they wanted to get to the big compound. They had to do what was asked of them, earn some trust. He nodded at Hilly, taking a spoonful of the stew, urging her to do the same with a look.

The concern didn't leave her face, but she took a bite. They ate in companionable silence, Free munching on some of the scraps a woman had given him outside the tent.

When he was just about finished, the man who'd led them here reappeared making no sound whatsoever.

"You'll come with me," he said with no preamble.

Cam stood, held out a hand for Hilly, but the man shook his head.

"She stays here. You come with me."

That gave Cam a pause. More than. He eyed the man. "I don't see any reason for that."

"You don't have to."

Cam took a few moments to tamp down his frustration, and the *"hell no"* he wanted to spit in the man's direction. He wasn't going to be separated from Hilly, but he had to be careful. Strategic.

"Look," Cam said, trying to find some measure of calm over fury. "I'm not going anywhere without my wife until I have some reason to trust any of you. I may want to be one of you because of your group's ideals, but I don't know you as men or women yet."

The man remained completely unperturbed, and completely unmoved. "To be one of us, you'll need to come with me. And she'll need to stay here."

Cam clenched his jaw in an effort to keep his mutinous words to himself. If he could remain calm, he could reason with this man. He wasn't letting Hilly out of his sight, that was for sure.

Except, he felt her hand close over his and squeeze. He glanced at her and she was staring at him imploringly.

"You should go, Cameron. This is your

dream," she said, raising her eyebrows as if encouraging him to remember why they were here. She flicked a glance at the intimidating jerk currently trying to wedge them apart. "I can take care of myself. I'll help these nice women clean up after our lunch. And Free will be with me." She squeezed his hand, hard, a clear sign the end result was more important than this moment.

She wanted her father back, and the best chance they had at that was infiltrating this group—not at their fake, near-empty decoy camp, but at the main compound, wherever it was.

He took a breath, tried to blow out the frustration and the gut feeling that leaving her alone was wrong. All wrong.

But she'd said she could take care of herself. He should believe her on that score.

"All right," he acquiesced, looking at Hilly instead of the man he was supposed to go with. He was making too much of this. Likely the man wanted to question them separately to make sure their stories matched up. The Protectors were a group wanted by the government. They couldn't be too careful with strangers who could potentially be undercover FBI or ATF.

So, this was just their routine and Cam

had to accept it. Trust Hilly to handle herself, and be smart enough to ace whatever test this was.

But before he followed this strange man who knew where to be tested on who knew what, he leaned down to Hilly. He brushed his mouth over her cheek, trying to keep any *feeling* that small contact elicited caged away.

"Be careful," he whispered, letting his palm drift over the crown of her hair before he stood to his full height and followed the man in charge without looking back.

He was afraid all this *feeling* jangling around inside of him would show on his face, would change things he couldn't afford to change right now. He could stand the threat of danger if they were together, but being separated?

It was like a jagged, searing slice of a blade against his chest. More so because he had no choice. This was the only possible route to take right now. Following the man on a narrow, rocky trail away from the camp.

Cam watched the man's every move. He wouldn't be isolated and then taken out, not with Hilly waiting for him. The man might have a bigger, more dangerous gun within quicker reach than Cam's smaller, holstered weapon, but that was only one advantage.

"Cameron Tyler," the man said conversationally as they hiked farther and farther away from the camp. "Former military, I take it."

"Yes."

"Marines, if I had to guess."

Cam didn't let his discomfort at being made show. "You guess right."

"Why'd you leave?"

"I thought I could do more good at home. We've got a lot of problems in our own country." That lie was hard, certainly harder than pretending Hilly was his wife.

The man made a noncommittal sound, leading them up and up until he stopped on a rocky outcropping that looked out over a valley of open land. There weren't any structures out this way, just trees, fields and the ribbon of a river catching the sunlight every now and again down below.

It was beautiful, and Cam had a bad feeling this man hoped it was the last thing Cam ever saw. Too bad for the man, Cam wasn't going to go down easily.

But when Cam slid him a glance, the man only stared. He made no move to push him off the cliff or reach for his weapon. He stood. He studied. So, Cam let him.

Eventually, he spoke, his dark eyes never

once leaving Cam. "There's no record of you. Or your wife."

"Record?" Cam asked blankly while his brain tried to figure out just where this man had run the fake names he and Hilly had given him. He'd need to hack into a government system, which he supposed an antigovernment group might have the tools to do, but where? Had to be close. Unless he'd passed along the fake names to someone else.

Too many possibilities. Too many variables.

"Not a marriage license, not a driver's license with pictures that match your face. You two don't seem to exist. It'll take time to hack into your military records, but so far…" The man trailed off, threat laced in his tone.

The cold dread in Cam's stomach intensified, but he isolated that feeling away with all the rest. "We like staying off the grid. The government doesn't need to be tracking me. My military records…" He shrugged. "They'll say what they say."

Again, the man made that noncommittal sound. Then he patted the gun strapped to his back. "I will find out who you are."

A threat, in more ways than one. Cam shrugged again, being careful to make sure it wasn't as jerky and tense as he felt. "Go right ahead."

"You sure you don't want to give me the truth here and now? Save you a lot of trouble."

"You've got the truth. My name is Cameron."

"But not Tyler."

"I didn't say that."

"Didn't not say it either. So, Cameron, former Marine, Wyoming resident, fake husband. If I start digging into you, what do you think I'll find?"

Cam didn't consider himself a particularly quick-tempered man. He'd grown up a Delaney, and been expected to be the one to keep his temper in all situations, most especially volatile Carson situations. He always had. His career as a Marine had been *all* about controlling his temper and following orders and doing the right thing.

He'd been faced with far more irritants than a strange man threatening to look into his background, and yet he couldn't remember the last time he'd been this close to losing his temper.

"FBI? ATF? Maybe just local law enforcement on his own time trying to figure a case out."

Cam laughed, and he didn't have to pretend

he found that amusing. "Strike three, you're out, buddy."

"I don't know who you are, or what you think you're doing, but let me give you a clear warning—you don't want to get involved in this. Take your friend back to wherever you came from and stay there."

"My wife."

"I don't have much experience with wives, but they generally don't look like they're going to jump out of their skin when their husband kisses them on the cheek."

Cam tried to ignore the tide of embarrassment that swept through him at that. He'd needed an excuse to get his mouth close enough to whisper an assurance to her, but he hadn't considered the move might read as unwanted all over her face.

He'd lost his touch and was making mistakes all over the place, and Hilly and her father were going to pay the price.

*Sound familiar?*

Aaron dead. His family left with that weight of loss, such pointless loss.

"It'd be better if you tell me what you are. FBI?"

When Cam didn't say anything, the man looked out over the ledge, a sharp, frustrated expression on his face. Something about that struck Cam as all wrong.

In fact, this whole exchange did. The man had made him out as not who he said he was, but there were no threats. Violence didn't simmer in the air. The man seemed more disappointed Cam had lied to him about his name than anything menacing.

It didn't add up.

The man crossed his arms over his chest and glared at Cam, though the lack of threatening force still baffled Cam altogether.

"Better for you if you tell me," the man said gruffly. "It's not like we kill government agents out here. We don't need that kind of trouble. You're not in danger if you 'fess up. We'd just send you on your way."

Which was not the kind of messages that had been coded into everything Cam had read about the Protectors. They hated the government—most especially the agencies that had tried to infiltrate them and bring them down. They believed in protection *at all costs*. Cam assumed that meant violence and, yes, even murder.

Something was off here, in more ways than one. "And just why would you care what's better for me?"

The man's expression sharpened, and whatever he'd been thinking about that had caused him to seem frustrated was gone. The blank, weapon-like exterior was back in place.

"I don't. You and your lady friend want to get chewed up and spit out, no skin off my nose. Figured I'd give you a chance to be smart."

"Smartest thing I can do is become a Protector. Protect what's mine. That's what I'm after."

The man rolled his eyes, as if he didn't take the Protector group seriously at all. Or maybe he was simply rolling his eyes at Cam's lie.

"Take you back now," he said, immediately moving back where they came from.

"But I—"

The man was out of earshot, long mean strides meant to put distance between them. Cam followed him, though he paid attention to the trail. If there was a trail here, it led somewhere other than just that cliff. It would be worth exploring later.

The man might have figured out Cam had given him a fake name, but he was looking in all the wrong corners. FBI and the like. He'd be busy trying to prove Cam was with a government agency and finding absolutely nothing.

It would give Cam time to poke around,

gather more information about the group that might help them infiltrate it once they made it to the main compound. Surely when they found he had no ties to the government, they'd trust him.

He took the last curve of the trail and the tents came into view, the man quite a few yards ahead of him, though Cam was under no illusion the man didn't know exactly how far he was and exactly what he'd do if Cam bolted.

He didn't understand this little interlude, but the lack of threats eased his mind to an extent.

Until he got within a few yards of the lean-to, and Hilly wasn't there. Free wasn't either. Cold fear skittered up his spine, but it was a foolish panic. She'd likely just gone back to the tent they'd been given.

"Where is she?" the man barked.

The three women cleaning and cooking didn't so much as jump at the harsh tone, but Cam was immediately put on alert. Why was this man worried about where Hilly was? Why didn't he *know*?

One of the women looked up at the man with blank eyes and her fake warm smile. "Where is who?"

# Chapter Thirteen

Hilly never thought she'd prefer the man who'd led them on the punishing hike to the decoy camp, but in the face of the burly man with a gun trained on her chest, she missed him a whole heck of a lot.

She bumped along in some all-terrain vehicle, hands tied behind her back with something hard and plastic that bit into her skin. The driver had been the one to tie her up and throw her in here. Burly gun guy had been holding his weapon trained on her ever since he'd materialized in the lean-to.

The women had done nothing. They'd gone on as if they hadn't even noticed two men grabbing her, overpowering her and taking her away. They'd chatted and cleaned as if no one else existed.

Hilly hoped she lived long enough to spit in their faces.

As much as the gun unnerved her, especially with the intense bumping of the vehicle as they drove too fast over rocky ground, she held on to the belief that she had a chance to survive. After all, if they wanted her dead they clearly could have done it back at the lean-to. Those women hadn't cared.

Her true worry, one she kept trying to push away lest it made her cry, was that the man had lured Cam away to harm him. Cam could be dead or injured, just like her father could be.

She closed her eyes. Tears threatened. Hopelessness threatened. But the bottom line was they could be dead, sure, but they could just as easily be alive. It was all fifty-fifty happenstance, and the only way she found out for sure was if she lived.

So, she would. She would stay alive, and she would do what Cam had tasked her with: observe. Pay attention. File it all away. If she did that she could find her father, find Cam *and* escape this situation.

They'd said they were taking her to the compound to "await trial." She didn't know what that meant, but as the vehicle kept moving down the mountain, it didn't seem to be taking the same confusing, circular route the other man had hiked her and Cam up. This was a straight shot to lower altitudes.

That was good. As long as they didn't keep going too long, the decoy camp wouldn't be too far away.

She tried to count the seconds and keep track of the minutes. The separation with Cam was scary and not at all ideal, but if these men brought her to the main compound she had a chance to find her father.

That was her primary goal. All others were secondary, no matter how often her mind drifted to Cam and if he was all right. Cam could take care of himself. He'd been a Marine. Surely that meant he could hold his own.

The vehicle slowed and Hilly held her breath. They'd been in the car maybe ten minutes. Could they really be this close?

She craned her neck, trying to get a glimpse of where they were headed instead of where they'd been. The man with the gun didn't seem to care, so she kept looking, kept noting things like the cluster of trees, the abnormally shaped boulder. Anything that would help her find this place again if she escaped.

When the vehicle pulled through that cluster of trees, she nearly gasped. There were tents and lean-tos like at the decoy camp, but at least twenty of the weird square tents, and two giant lean-tos, along with a third building that reminded her of her cabin, though bigger.

The vehicle stopped in front of it and the driver hopped out. He grabbed her, pulling her over the side, while the man with the gun followed—always pointing that awful thing right at her.

The driver pushed her forward so harshly she nearly fell, but he grabbed her before she did, yanking her back up and sending a shooting pain through the joints of her shoulder at the odd angle of her arms. She cried out at the shock of it.

"Shut up," the man hissed in her ear.

He kept nudging her toward the door of the cabin, though he was gentler now. She got the impression he wanted to hurt her, but was holding himself back.

But why?

The man knocked on the door, and she filed away in her brain the way he did it. Two short raps, then a loud bang with the flat of his hand. After a pause, he did it again, and she wished she'd thought to count the seconds of the pause. But it was more important to remember the things that mattered rather than beat herself up over the things she couldn't keep track of.

The door creaked open. Inside was dark, despite the light of day outside, and Hilly's body rejected the possibility of going into this shadowy, dank, dungeon-like abyss. She tried to step backward, lean or twist away, anything but be forced inside.

But there were two big men behind her, and eventually they maneuvered her into the darkness.

This was the most panicked she'd felt the whole time. Being tied up, being taken somewhere against her will wasn't a picnic, but the darkness had panic crawling through her veins, terror roiling through her stomach.

"Please," she gasped through breaths that were harder and harder to take.

When a light flicked on, she flinched against the sudden brightness. One of the men holding her arm chuckled, then they were pulling her forward, and she forced her eyes open, forced herself to observe, to watch.

It was one big room inside the cabin, set up like an old-fashioned church. She'd seen pictures of churches in different textbooks or articles. Pews lined the sides, an aisle in the middle, but it led to a long table, with three men seated on the other side.

They'd said trial, and while the seating was church-like, she decided that was not what this was. It was a courtroom.

"Will you please state your name?" one of the men said, holding a pen in one hand.

She looked around wildly. But there were only the two men holding her, and the three men behind the desk asking her calm questions.

"State your name, please," the man repeated, his voice still calm but lined with steel.

"L-Leigh. Leigh Tyler. My name is Leigh Tyler."

He wrote something down, conferred with the men on either side of him, then nodded. "We'll ask one more time. State your real name."

"I just told y—"

Almost simultaneously with the man's sharp nod, she felt a sharp, punishing blow to the back of her knees. She fell to the ground on a yelp of surprise and pain, both from the blow and the way her knees hit the hard ground.

"Are you ready to tell us your real name?"

Hilly squeezed her eyes shut, focused on the cool of the dirt underneath her palms rather than the throbbing pain in her knees. She swallowed, breathed and then opened her eyes, looking straight at the man asking the questions.

"My name is Leigh Tyler."

Again he nodded, and again she was hit

with something hard and painful, this time against her back. She tried to bite back the cry, but it was too painful. Too much.

"Another chance," the man said, so calm and untouched by any of this.

She struggled to breathe and she couldn't decide what was worse: the pain or the truth. But if it were Cam in this situation, and it was very possible he was somewhere else in the same exact situation or a worse one, he would take the pain. He wouldn't break, not if it put her at risk.

She knew that, beyond a shadow of a doubt, so she braced for the next blow and repeated her fake name.

She waited for the blow, but it never came. Eventually she opened her eyes, looking up at the men behind the table. Did they believe her now?

But the man was smiling pleasantly, and Hilly didn't think that boded well.

"If pain won't sway you, perhaps this will." He made a gesture, and the man to his left got up and went to a door in the back of the cabin. He opened the door, and motioned someone inside.

A small man, head bowed, shuffled in, someone behind him pushing him forward. His hands were tied behind his back much like hers, and she could tell despite his down-ward-cast face there were bruises across his cheek and neck.

He was pushed forward, something harsh ordered at him and he finally looked up. When he locked eyes with Hilly she had to swallow a gasp, swallow the word that wanted to come out of her mouth.

*Dad. Dad. Oh, God, Dad.*

"Recognize each other?" the man behind the table asked, something like pleasure rippling through his voice.

"N-no," Hilly said firmly, hoping her father would back her up. She swallowed at the bile rising in her throat. She couldn't let panic or terror win. "Are you going to do that to me?" she whispered, hoping it would make them think she was only scared of being the next—not because she recognized her father.

Dad. *Dad.* He was bloody and bruised, but he was alive. She wanted to cry, weep with relief, and she couldn't let herself.

She had to focus, and think, and somehow get them both out of here.

"I told you," Dad said, his voice sounding raspy and abused. "I don't know what you're talking about. I killed the girl like you told me to all those years ago. I don't know who this is."

Killed the girl?

"Our intelligence says otherwise, brother."

The way the man said *brother* made Hilly's skin crawl, but she grabbed on to Dad's story.

"I don't know who he is. I don't know who you are. I just want to go back to my husband. Please." She didn't look at her father, hoped he had the good sense not to react to that.

"Your husband," the man said with a little chuckle. "Cameron Tyler."

"Yes. Yes, please. He's okay, isn't he? Can I see him? Can't you just let me go? Please. I'm only here because he wanted to join you guys."

The man made a considering noise, and when she dared look up at him, his gaze was on her father. She couldn't risk looking at him, as well. She might fall apart, or he might.

"Does the name Hillary Simmons ring any bells to you, young lady?"

Ice settled low in her gut and spread up her spine, just like when Laurel had said the name Hillary—was that only two days ago? She kept her gaze steady, thinking about Cam and what he would do in this situation.

Remain calm. Stay as close to the truth as she could. File it all away to use later. "It doesn't. I told you, my name is Leigh Tyler. I just want to go back to my husband."

"Where did you meet your husband, Mrs. Tyler?" he asked pleasantly enough, though he said *Mrs. Tyler* with the kind of sarcasm that made it clear he didn't believe her.

*Stay close to the truth, just like we practiced.* "The police station, believe it or not."

"And what were you doing at the police station?"

*Stay close to the truth. Remember the plan.* It was her mantra now. Her center of calm. "He was reporting a crime. I was visiting a friend." They'd agreed to stay close to the truth, without giving away she might have been reporting Dad missing. Flip their roles, be vague about the crime.

"You have a *friend* at *what* police station exactly?"

Her gaze sharpened on this man, who apparently thought she was stupid enough to give him more ammunition to use against her. "I'm not telling you that while you have me tied up and have no concern over physically attacking me. I won't bring my friend or my hometown into whatever this is. You're a madman."

The man's smile spread. "Suit yourself." Once again, he conferred with the man next to him, their whispers too low to make out any words.

The other man, who hadn't spoken at all, got to his feet and went over to the man holding Dad. He whispered something in his ear, and the man nodded. Then he walked over to the men behind her.

Hilly shook, and she didn't try to stop herself now. They'd expect her to be afraid, wouldn't they? Why not let her actual fear show through when Leigh Tyler, stranger to all this, here only because her husband wanted to join the Protectors, would definitely be horrifically afraid?

He whispered something to the man who'd driven them here, and the driver nodded. He did the same to the man who'd continually trained the gun on her. Each man grabbed an arm and hauled her to her feet, then started dragging her toward the back door.

Dad was already being led out by the man who'd brought him in. In complete silence, they were taken to a tiny building behind the first. It looked much like the cabin she'd just been in, but there were no windows.

Greasy panic crawled through her and the *"please, no"* was out of her mouth before she could think to fight it back. "Don't. Please."

But they tossed Dad inside, and then her.

It was pitch-black, and she heard the sound of locks clicking in the doors. She was standing, hands tied behind her back, in a small, stuffy, black space.

"No. No. No." She didn't think she could take this. For a blinding moment of panic she opened her mouth to yell out exactly who she was.

"Shh," Dad said quietly. "It'll be okay."

She thought of Cam telling her that. Things were *not* okay.

Except Dad was alive, and they were together.

"Tell me, Mrs. Tyler, how'd you end up here?" he asked loudly, a clear hint she was supposed to keep pretending.

She swallowed, tried to calm her breathing, her heart. Her legs ached and tears were spilling over, but she was alive and Dad was alive, and Cam was somewhere out there and it was possible he could save them if they couldn't save themselves. It had to be possible.

"My husband read about the Protectors. He wanted to join them. So, I came with him. We were going to join them." She paused, taking another deep, calming breath and letting it out. "What's your name?"

There was a pause. "James Adams."

It was the name she'd always known her

father to use. The name there was no matching record of. Hilly frowned, but she kept on. "How did you come to be here?" she asked, hoping that even in lies she could find some truths.

"I've been a member of the Protectors since the seventies," Dad said carefully. "But I haven't lived at the compound since the eighties. It was too confining. I wanted my own space, but I still came back for meetings."

That could be a truth. Clearly the Protectors knew who Dad was, knew the name James Adams, so most of what he told her could be the truth. She had to hope in the truth she could find some potential for escape.

"If you're a member, why are they treating you this way?"

"They think I've betrayed them."

"How?" she demanded, wincing at how desperate she sounded.

"They seem to think... They think instead of killing an enemy's daughter as they tasked me with years ago, as I *accomplished* years ago," he said firmly. "They think I kept her and secretly raised her as my own instead."

Hilly didn't breathe. There was a buzzing sound in her ears, a slow-blooming pain in her chest.

*Raised her as my own.*
*Hillary Simmons. Hillary.*
*Raised her as my own.*

"Breathe," Dad whispered, something like regret laced in that very simple word.

Still, she did as she was told. She sucked in air, let it raggedly out, and she swallowed down all the words scrambling for purchase, desperate to escape.

*I can't be her. I can't be.*

## Chapter Fourteen

The man was barking orders and demands at the women, but they kept placidly insisting they didn't know what he was talking about. Like Hilly had never existed.

Cam had the fleeting thought they'd helped her escape, and that was why they were lying to both Cam himself and the man angrily demanding answers.

Except it didn't make sense. Hilly wouldn't leave him. Not without some kind of message.

Cam stepped forward to make his own demands and threats, but suddenly thought better of it. They weren't going to give him answers. He needed to find Hilly. Which meant he needed to ditch all these people.

While the man and women were occupied in their argument, Cam slowly walked farther and farther away as he scanned the area. There weren't footprints in the dusty floor of the lean-to; it had seemingly been swept—which of course was suspicious.

But as he edged his way to the side of the lean-to, he did see footprints. His and the man's from their going earlier, a few smaller prints he was pretty sure belonged to the women in the lean-to and ones that held his attention—paw prints.

He followed them, not bothering to pay attention to the people arguing in the lean-to. Wherever they'd taken Hilly, they'd covered up the tracks, or simply not left any, but Free was another story.

Had the dog run off after Hilly? Had she simply wandered before Hilly was taken? There were a myriad of what-ifs, but it was the best lead he had, so he followed it.

He nearly lost the trail three times through rocks and brush before he came to a small grassy area. There were still Free's tracks in places, but there were also vehicle tracks—new ones if he had to guess, since the wind hadn't messed with the clear flattening of grass and brush. If Hilly had been taken, especially against her will, he had to believe it was in that vehicle.

He glanced around the area, seeing no sign of anyone following him. Hoping he wasn't outing himself, he let out a sharp whistle. He began to follow the vehicle tracks, whistling or saying "Free" into the wind as he went.

He wasn't sure how far he'd gone when he first spotted Free running toward him. Her fur was covered in mud, and she was panting. She barked once, trotting back the way she'd come and up to him with another bark.

"Almost there, girl," he murmured, trusting the dog to take him down the right path. Besides, between the dog and the tire tracks, all things pointed to Hilly having been taken this way.

As long as the vehicle had driven over grassy or muddy areas, he'd be able to follow the tracks even if Free lost the scent—or whatever dog intuition she had to lead Cam where he needed to go. He took off after Free on a jog.

He ran as fast as he could, having no idea how far away they would have taken Hilly, or how lost he was going to be. He didn't have his pack or any supplies aside from the gun strapped to his waist.

While he ran, he worked through the problem. It was possible the Protectors had purposefully separated them to question them and make sure they were who they said they were. It was possible.

But.

The thing that bothered Cam on a deep, uneasy level was how the man had seemed so surprised, so outraged that Hilly was gone. Clearly he hadn't been in on the plan, and he thought he should be.

Nothing added up, but it didn't have to. The most important thing right now was finding Hilly. Then they could try to figure out the math.

The faint sound of an engine had Cam pausing, even as Free barked at him, as if urging him forward. "Stay," he ordered the dog, straining to hear which way the sound was coming from.

He looked around him, but there wasn't much cover. A few rocks here and there, but he was mostly in open land. He swore, then moved toward the rocks. He did his best to position himself and Free between the rocks and the sound of that engine.

The engine got closer and closer, and Cam kept his eyes on Free, whispering all the quiet commands he could think of.

The engine cut, and Cam kept completely still. This wasn't good. Wasn't good at all. He shifted slightly, trying to reach for his weapon, but boots came into view.

Keeping his hand at his side, slowly inching it back toward his holster, Cam looked up at the man who'd separated him from Hilly.

"Where the hell do you think you're going?" the man demanded.

"Where the hell do you think? To find my wife, who apparently doesn't exist." He kept his gaze on the man, all the while reaching for the weapon.

The man scowled and looked around the clearing, then dark eyes turned back to him, snapping with frustration. "I want her real name."

Cam snorted. "If my wife had a fake name, I certainly wouldn't give you her real one."

"I thought you wanted to be a Protector."

"I do."

"But you don't trust me?"

"No. I know what I read about the Protectors and what they stand for, but I don't even know you're one of them. All I know is I came back and suddenly everyone is pretending my wife doesn't exist. You'll have to pardon my skepticism at anything you or those women have to say. I'm not even sure I believe you are who you say you are."

There was a violent glint in the man's eye, but he didn't reach for his gun, which was still strapped to his back. Cam figured he could at least reach his in the same amount of time it would take this man to get to his. They'd likely shoot each other and bleed out in the middle of nowhere.

It was a depressing thought, one that had his hand stopping its move toward the gun. He'd stay alert, stay ready, but actually shooting the man and escaping was unlikely as of yet.

"What if your wife isn't who she says she is?" the man said, slowly folding his arms over his chest.

"Who else would she be?"

"The name Hillary Simmons mean anything to you?"

Simmons. Hillary was the name Laurel had said was on the tape, but she hadn't mentioned Simmons. Ethan had been the other name they'd been able to hear. "No," Cam said truthfully. "If you think my wife is her, I can guarantee you you're wrong."

"How can you guarantee me?"

"Huh?"

"How long have you known each other?"

Cam could have lied. He should have lied, and quickly, but this line of questioning threw him off. The fact the man hadn't dragged him back to camp, and had seemed baffled and irritated by Hilly's disappearance in the face of the women back at the decoy camp, only confused Cam more.

"Who are you? Really?" Cam demanded.

The man made the same snorting noise Cam had made earlier. "I know where she is. I know where they have her. What I don't know is why."

"You think I do?"

"I think you know something. Something you're not giving me." He ran an irritable hand through his hair. "What law enforcement agency are you with?"

"I told you. I'm not with any agency."

"I know you're not who you say. You might as well tell me the truth."

The thing Cam couldn't figure, in a long line of unfigurable things, was that the man had a weapon strapped to him and wasn't using it to threaten or force answers. It was possible he knew Cam was armed and didn't want to end up in the whole bleeding-to-death scenario, but the man hadn't even grabbed for the gun.

Cam stood, and when the man still didn't grab for his gun, Cam didn't hesitate to take a threatening step forward. "If you've hurt her—"

"They won't have hurt her. Yet."

Cam couldn't understand the faint line of

concern on the man's forehead. He had to be kidding himself. It wasn't concern. Couldn't be.

But he did understand he had said *you*, and the man had said *they*. Maybe it was reading too far into things, but that seemed telling. It didn't put him at any kind of ease, because he didn't know what kind of allegiances this man had, who the men who had Hilly were or anything.

All he knew was he had to get Hilly. He had to figure a way out of this. Cam thought briefly of rushing the man, but again, there was too much potential for them both to do a whole lot of damage to each other and end up dead. He had to be strategic.

He took a step back, and then another. The man rolled his eyes. "You're not running again."

"You going to stop me?" Cam nodded to the gun.

"I'm not going to shoot you," the man grumbled. "I don't want to hurt you *or* your wife."

"Then what do you want?"

"Justice," the man said, nearly under his breath. He jerked his chin toward the four-wheeler he'd ridden up on. "You want to find your wife, you're going to have to come with me."

"I can find her just fine on my own."

"No, you can't," the man said flatly. "And I can't let you. So, your choices are come with me or I tie you up and take you back to the camp you were just at to let those vulture women do what they want with you."

*Like hell.*

The man let out a sharp whistle and Free nearly jumped over the rock. "In," the man ordered, and Free followed the order, hopping into the bed of the four-wheeler.

Cam could not believe his eyes. "Free," he commanded, but the dog stayed resolutely in this stranger's vehicle.

"If you want to see your wife, I suggest you follow the dog's example."

Cam scowled, eyed the four-wheeler, the world around him and thought about his own internal clock. Hilly had been gone forty-five minutes at most, twenty-five minutes at least. He had to get to her. This man had a vehicle and knew where he was going. He also, supposedly, didn't want to hurt him or Hilly.

On an oath, and then a prayer that he wasn't totally miscalculating, Cam strode over and got in the seat next to the man. "You got a name?" he asked gruffly as the engine roared to life again.

"You can call me Zach."

TIME TICKED BY in unidentifiable terms and Hilly felt herself slowly stumbling toward insanity. The dark. The heavy, stale air that seemed to suck as much oxygen from her as it gave. Her father's labored breathing, and some awful truth blooming in the middle of it.

*They think I kept her and secretly raised her as my own instead.*

Dad hadn't said anything since then, and though she had a million questions for him, there were men outside. Anyone could be listening. And worse, so much worse, she didn't want to know.

*They think I kept her and secretly raised her as my own instead.*

The words were a constant loop, making her question everything, including if any of this was actually happening or if it was just a very vivid dream.

She felt something brush against her, winced away until she heard Dad's gentle shush. "Why are you here?" he whispered, so low she had to strain and think to make out the words.

"For you."

"Leave me."

"How can I do that?" she choked out, the fear clogging her throat making it harder to whisper. "You're all I have. They burned down the cabin."

"No. That wasn't them."

"What?"

Dad sighed. "Can't explain."

"You have to explain," she replied, too loud she knew, but she needed answers. Her life as she knew it was completely upended and she needed to know how and why, so she could... So she could... Something. Do something that would make sense if she understood this.

She thought about Cam. Was he okay? If he was, he'd be trying to find her. Would he get himself hurt in the process? She knew he'd do whatever it took to find her, to save her. It was who he was.

She realized, with a sickening roll of her gut, she didn't know that about her father, or whoever this man was. She didn't know what he believed, who he was loyal to. She understood nothing about it.

How could she be so in the dark about the man who'd raised her, and be so certain about a man she'd only known a few days?

Maybe if she had more energy she'd talk herself out of that, but tied up and in grave danger, she could only trust her gut.

"We have to find a way to get you out of here," Dad whispered.

Cam would get her out of here. She didn't know why she believed that, why it seemed impossible he could be hurt and incapacitated like her. But she could only trust that—

Clanging metal stopped her thoughts, and she moved toward the sound. Something thumped, and then a door opened—not the door they'd been pushed in either. This was to the back.

Just a sliver of light shone through as it opened a crack. Hilly tried to think how she could fight off anyone with her arms tied behind her back. Her boots were hard, and with enough leverage she could deliver a hard kick and—

"Hilly?"

"Cam." Her knees nearly gave out as she moved for the light.

Before she could figure out how, Cam was inside, pulling her to him. He held her to his chest. It was only a brief second, but she felt his relief. She felt his *care*. Dad had told her not to trust the outside world, but he'd also told her she was his daughter. He'd kept her isolated and in the dark.

Cam had given her choices. Cam had trusted her, and she couldn't help but trust him in return. She didn't question him. She wouldn't.

"Come on," he said, taking her elbow and pulling her toward that light.

Hilly pulled away. "Someone will see you. They'll shoot."

"I've got a diversion going, but we only have five safe minutes. Come on." He bent over and pulled a knife out of his boot. Quickly, he cut the ties on her arms and started leading her to the door.

"Cam. Wait. My father." She looked back at where he stood in the corner, bruised and stoic. "We can't leave him."

Cam's expression was grim, but she couldn't let that stop her.

"Please." She gripped his shirt, ignoring the pain and ache in her wrists and arms. "Please, Cam. He's hurt. I…" She looked at her father in the swath of light. "I think they'll kill him."

"I'll stay," Dad said firmly.

"She wants you to go. You'll go," Cam replied. There was something hard in his voice she didn't recognize.

"I don't know who you are, boy, but—"

Cam crossed over to her father then, and without another word or argument, cut the ties on his wrists. Then he pushed him toward the door. "Let's go."

"I'm not going with you."

"Dad. Please. We don't have time for this. We have to get out of here."

Some unknown war raged on her father's face as he studied her. He jerked a chin toward Cam. "Who is he?"

"He's the man who saved me when you left me helpless and alone," Hilly shot back, tears stinging her eyes. "I know you're used to calling the shots, but you're the one who got us into this mess. So now? You'll do as we say."

"Just leave me," Dad said wearily. "Save yourselves."

"Not today," Cam said, nudging her father toward the door again. "Hilly. You're first. You have to run. Straight west, just follow the sun. Run and don't stop."

"But—"

He grabbed her by the arms, squeezing. "You have to, Hilly." He was so fiercely serious. "We have to get you out of here. Nothing adds up the way it should, which means we need to get you far, far away. They think you're someone else. I need you to run. I'll follow with your dad."

She wanted to tell Cam what Dad had said, but there was no time as Cam shook his head and gave her a nudge out the door. "Run. Don't stop. Don't look back. Just run. We'll be as close behind you as we can be. Free's out there at the tree line. She'll protect you."

*I want you to protect me.*

But she couldn't indulge that want right now. She nodded sharply, and stepped into the threshold of the door. She waited for Cam's signal, and when he said, *"Go,"* she took off.

He'd told her not to look back, but she couldn't help herself. Cam could outrun her, and yet she could feel him losing ground.

She glanced back once. Dad was struggling, huffing and puffing and running with a bit of a limp, but Cam stayed behind him, as if protecting him from anything that might come from the compound.

Something big and sweet bloomed in her chest, a wave of affection for the man who'd put himself at risk to protect someone simply because she'd asked him to.

She decided to let that feeling grow, wallow in it instead of the burning in her lungs as she faced forward again, upping her pace to the limits her body could endure.

No shots rang out. No one came running after them. Hilly wanted to believe that meant they were free. That everything would be okay from here on out.

But she knew it wasn't true.

## Chapter Fifteen

Cam had hoped to get farther, but even at a walk now he was afraid Hilly's father was going to keel over.

"Let's take a break," he offered.

"Not on my account," the man huffed in return.

"On all our accounts." Cam stopped, pulling Hilly onto a rock. Free whimpered and curled up at her feet. They all needed water, but they wouldn't be able to get any until they got to their destination.

"Dad, sit," Hilly implored, and the man finally took a seat next to her on the rock.

Cam pulled the map Zach had given him out of his pocket. It looked like they had a few miles to go yet before they reached the cabin Zach had assured him would be a safe place to stay.

It didn't sit right with Cam. It was still hard to trust Zach entirely, even though he had orchestrated the escape by calling an emergency meeting at the compound. And they'd escaped. Here they were, all three of them safe and sound.

Was Zach?

He shook his head. Hilly was his prime concern, and because her father was her prime concern, Cam had to care about the two of them over anyone else.

"Quick break, then back to walking. We're heading for a small cabin, so you'll want to keep an eye out. Best to get there before dark."

"Whose cabin?" Hilly asked, scratching Free behind the ears.

"The man who helped us escape. This is going to sound a little strange, but the guy who found us earlier today? He helped me. I don't know that I trust him fully, but he didn't want to hurt us. He led me to you, and he created the diversion so we could escape." Cam let out a breath. "None of this makes sense," he muttered. It rankled, but his focus had to be getting them to safety. Then he could work it out. Once Hilly was tucked away and *safe*.

"You shouldn't have stuck your nose in it," Hilly's father muttered irritably.

In the daylight, Cam could see how badly he'd been hurt. Which was the only thing that kept Cam from making his own snide comment. He glanced at Hilly. Okay, not the only thing. He'd do just about anything for Hilly.

The intensity of that feeling was concerning, but he didn't have time to dwell on it. "We should get back to it if we're going to make it before sundown." He held out a hand to Hilly and helped her up off the rock.

"There will be food and water and supplies there. So, we just have to grit it out a few more miles."

Hilly didn't withdraw her hand from his. Instead she leaned against him on a sigh. She was exhausted—physically and no doubt mentally. She needed comfort and he so desperately wanted to be the one to give it to her.

He brushed his mouth across her temple. It felt…necessary. Right to give her that physical comfort. Even if it wasn't. "You're holding up like a champ," he murmured.

She leaned harder, sighing against his neck. God, what he wouldn't give for some non-dangerous time with this woman.

On a deep breath, she straightened, seeming to draw some strength from him. Which pleased him far too much. "All right. Let's get going," she said with a nod to her father.

The man was still sitting, glaring at Cam. Which didn't concern Cam much, considering the man was the reason they were in this mess. Maybe he could learn a thing or two about how to take care of his daughter.

Cam looked forward, focusing on the task at hand. He consulted the map once more before heading out across the rocky, uneven ground. The primary objective was safety before sundown. So, he kept them headed west. He noted the landmarks Zach had outlined for him, and then, with the sun nearly gone, the cabin appeared on a rocky rise.

No one said anything. They just kept up their grim hiking until they reached the door. Cam counted the boards, up then over, just as Zach had instructed, then pulled a key out of a small indentation between the boards.

Cam unlocked the door and stepped inside first.

Inside, the cabin was small but cozy. There was a case of water bottles in the corner of the tiny galley kitchen and Cam pointed to it.

"Hydrate," he demanded, already searching the cupboards for a bowl for Free while Hilly handed her father a bottle and then one to Cam. Cam poured half of his in the metal bowl he'd found and put it on the floor for Free.

The dog drank greedily, and Cam finished his own bottle off in no time flat. Hilly and her father sipped theirs, both eyeing the cabin suspiciously.

There was a living area off to the side of the kitchen, then two doors—both open to show a tiny bathroom and a small bedroom mostly taken up by a bed.

When Hilly's gaze met his, she looked at him a little helplessly. Except she wasn't helpless. She was getting through all of this as though she was trained for intense physical demands, confusing, dangerous situations and even attacks on her person.

Because the idea of anyone laying a hand on her made him white-hot with rage, he compartmentalized that thought and emotion away. He'd deal with it later, when there was time to be angry. Right now it would only get him, and more important, Hilly, in trouble.

"What now?" she asked quietly.

"We wait." He didn't tell her that if Zach didn't appear by morning, Cam was going back for him. That could wait. "We'll spend the night here and decide what to do in the morning."

"They'll come after me," Hilly's father said gruffly.

Cam nodded. "Undoubtedly, but I left behind some confusing clues that should keep them busy elsewhere, at least for a while."

He and Zach had laid fake tracks back to the vehicle Zach had used to bring them to the compound.

He could only hope they followed those tracks rather than search the back of the building and find the other real ones and that the encroaching dark would halt their efforts.

"We'll eat and then we'll take turns sleeping, always having two people on lookout. We won't take any chances. Once we get back to Bent we can figure out the whys. For tonight, we rest, we recharge and we prepare to get home in one piece."

"I'll figure out the food," Hilly said, moving for the kitchen. "Both of you sit."

Cam wanted to argue with her, but he also wanted to talk to James out of her earshot. He pointed to the small living room area in the far corner—a chair and a couch arranged around a fireplace.

Cam decided to get the fire going as the evening would be cold. Since it was getting dark, the smoke wouldn't be visible as long as he put it out before sunrise. "Maybe you'd like to fill me in on your connection to the Protectors," he offered, picking a few logs from the stack on the floor.

"Maybe I wouldn't."

Cam eyed the man who'd settled himself

into the chair. He looked exhausted, beaten. And pissed.

"It would help me keep your daughter safe if you filled me in on what I'm dealing with here."

"Who asked you to keep her safe?"

"Someone needs to care enough to." He picked up a long match from a box on the mantel and lit the fire.

Something fired in the man's eyes, warning and violence, but exhaustion seemed to blank out both quickly enough. "You dragged her into this. God help you if you can't drag her out."

"No, James. You dragged her into it when you left her defenseless and alone," Cam replied, keeping his tone equitable.

James's face went mutinous, but he said nothing else. Which was good. Hilly didn't need to hear them have an extended argument. There was a time and a place for it, and Cam would make sure he had the opportunity. But it wasn't here.

He stoked the fire, letting the warmth of it seep into his skin and remind him how much walking he'd done today. Exhaustion threatened, but he pushed it away. James would take the first sleep rotation, then Hilly. Ideally, Zach would be back by then and they could decide what to do from there.

"Chili seemed to be the best choice out of the canned goods," Hilly said, moving into the living room. She handed her father a bowl and then him one. Hilly went back to the kitchen and returned with her own bowl before curling up next to Cam on the couch.

They ate around the fire in sleepy silence. If Cam could forget about everything else going on, it might even be nice. Maybe when this was all over he and Hilly could...

Well, thoughts for another time.

Once they'd eaten, Hilly collected the empty bowls. "Dad, you should rest. You're injured," she said.

"I'm—"

"Hurt," Hilly insisted. "Take a nap. We'll hold down the fort, and once you've slept some, we'll switch."

She moved to the kitchen and James grumbled as he got to his feet. He moved to the bedroom, though he shot Cam one killing look. "Keep your hands off my daughter," he muttered, then stepped into the room, Free at his heels. When they were both inside, he shut the door with a firm slap.

Cam sighed and got to his feet. He wasn't worried about the man's warning. He'd touch

Hilly if he damn well pleased, and, yes, he rather pleased. But now was not the time nor place.

Hilly moved into the living room, wringing her hands. Her worried glance was on the bedroom door.

"You don't think he'll make a run for it, do you?" Cam asked, only half kidding.

Hilly shook her head. "I'm not sure what he'd get out of that. They were going to kill him, Cam. I know they were."

Sympathy and affection wound so deeply inside of him it was hard not to stagger from it. He wanted to take that pain and fear away, and he couldn't.

*Just another failure.*

He swallowed at the pain lodged in his throat. All his failures on complete display, but Hilly looked over at him like he had the answers, and he wanted to. He wanted to be strong and the person she leaned on.

The only way he could be that was to get over the guilt. He hadn't thought that was in his control. Guilt existed, whether he wanted it to or not, but he realized in this moment as Hilly watched him that he'd used guilt for the past year as an excuse and a shield. Guilt was safe, because it meant you didn't have to accept you couldn't control everything.

He couldn't, though. He hadn't been able to control how Aaron felt about ending his life, and when Hilly was looking for answers he couldn't give her. He knew there was nothing he could have done then.

There was nothing he could do now. He couldn't control this situation he was in. He could only roll with it, react to what came and do everything in his power to get Hilly home safe.

He'd do his best for Hilly, and if it wasn't good enough… That was life.

He shuddered out a breath. Guilt didn't get a person anywhere. It held them back. That had been good enough in his first year out of the military, but it wasn't anymore.

Not with her standing there, needing him.

He gestured her to the couch, where she sat back down. He took the seat next to her. What he wanted to do was pull her into him, let her sleep against his shoulder and assure her everything would be okay.

He clasped his hands together behind his neck, staring at the fire. "If they wanted him dead, why is he still alive?"

She shook her head, but he could tell she knew something. Something she wasn't ready to tell him. He could see the marks on her wrists where they'd tied her up, and it reminded him to be patient. To give her space and time. They had that now.

Once Zach met them as he said he would later tonight, they'd be able to plan how to get back to Bent. They needed to make full use of this short respite.

"You should rest, too."

She shook her head. "Too wired. Too..." She shook her head again, but she moved closer to him on the cushion. She looked up at him, searching his face for something. If he knew what, he'd give it to her, but as it was, he just held that warm brown gaze.

She leaned into him with no warning and brushed her mouth over his. It shocked him, not just because it was so familiar when it shouldn't be, but because the small kiss rocketed through him like a meteor. Big and bright and changing.

His skin tingled with the contact, and his mouth was greedy for more, but he held himself back with that iron will he'd developed as a Marine.

"What was that for?" he managed to ask.

"I'm pretty sure the knight in shining armor always gets a kiss from the princess he saves." She smiled up at him, soft and sweet. "At least, that's what I always read."

He found himself smiling in spite of everything going on around them. "I think you're delirious."

"Probably," she agreed with a laugh. "But you could kiss me again just to be sure."

It was too tempting to resist. She wanted him to kiss her, was *hopeful* for it. In what world would he ever refuse that?

He dropped his mouth to hers, softer and slower than he might have been with another woman. But she wasn't timid. Unpracticed, maybe, but not timid at all. She met his mouth with hers, exploring with a curiosity that aroused him beyond measure.

Too much, too potent, and not just causing that iron tightening of his body, but clutching something deeper in his chest. In his heart.

Far too much to take, and yet far too much to resist.

She let out a shuddery sigh against his mouth and he had to remind himself Hilly had no experience with *people*, let alone men. Like this.

He opened his eyes, trying to center himself in the moment. In remembering that no matter how strong or in charge she appeared, she'd spent a lifetime sheltered away from the reality of life.

Slowly, she opened her eyes when he stopped. They were brown and luminous and it was hard to believe the truth of her being sheltered, because the woman with those eyes knew exactly what she was doing.

Or maybe he just wanted her to. "Hilly."

"I know," she said on an exhale. "It's not the time or place." She closed her eyes, and she let the exhaustion slump her body against him. She leaned into his shoulder, placing her hand over his galloping heart. "I just wanted to pretend like it was all over for a second."

Tempting, tempting to let her—to let himself. But not yet. "We're getting there." It was hard to think about what would come after, when there was so much in the here and now that didn't make sense, but eventually it'd be over. He'd just be Cam Delaney, and she'd just be Hilly Adams, and maybe those two people could…

"Is it always like that?" she asked, studying his face. "A kiss. Does it always feel like…"

"No. Not always." Never. Never had a kiss turned him inside out.

She rubbed her hand against his heart. "This is special. It feels special."

He closed his hand over it. *Special.* It seemed like a weak word, like a child's word, but whatever this was, this hard, twisting thing in his chest that felt like some mix of terror and elation, it was special, and it was important. "It is, Hilly. It is." He pulled her hand off his chest. "But—"

"But we're in the middle of danger." She sat up, off his shoulder, met his gaze. "That's the only thing holding you back, isn't it?"

Cam blew out a breath. "No. Not the only thing." He knew the next words would hurt her, but he also knew she needed to hear them. Maybe coming from him it wouldn't be so bad. He could hope. "Hilly, you don't know who you are."

# Chapter Sixteen

Those words hurt. For a second. But no matter the swirling confusion in her mind, Hilly rejected his words. She kept her gaze steady on his.

"I know exactly who I am." Maybe not fully, but to an extent. She knew the woman she wanted to be, even if she didn't know the things she wanted to do yet.

But she wanted Cam, and she wanted the truth. She'd have both eventually, but for now they'd focus on the truth. "He isn't my father. He told me, more or less. Whoever I am, it's not James Adams's daughter."

It was strange to say it out loud. To hear the words in her own voice. To accept it fully. She wasn't really his. She wasn't really *her*. Hilly Adams was a lie.

Her whole life, at least the part that she could remember, was a lie.

"Hilly?"

She looked up at Cam. The warmth of his hand holding hers reminded her where she was, who she was. "He's not… I don't know who is. I don't know why he had me. But the Protectors wanted me dead, I guess. When I was a baby. It had to have been when I was a baby. I remember being such a little thing, and James Adams was my father. I was Hilly. I remember…" She shook her head. She had to be focused, meticulous now. She could have an emotional response to all this later, when they weren't in danger. When she was home.

Home. She didn't have a home. She didn't have a home or a family. But Cam was holding her hand, and she hung on to that one connection.

"When we were locked in that building together, he insinuated that he was supposed to kill me, but he kept me instead."

She watched Cam's expression sharpen. He was putting pieces together. She didn't understand how he could look so in control, so unfazed and as though exhaustion wasn't everything this day was made of.

His hazel gaze met hers. "Hillary Simmons," he said.

Hilly swallowed at the name that caused a physical reaction inside of her, this name that had to be hers. "That was the name the man said. The man in the meeting room—that's where they took me first. They demanded to know who I was." She thought of the painful blows and decided not to share those with Cam. Not yet. "He asked if I recognized the name Hillary Simmons, but I didn't."

"But who is Hillary Simmons? Why did the Protectors want you dead?"

"I don't know." Tears threatened, but she blinked them away. Tears and sadness didn't change anything. "He won't talk about it. Dad won't... Even now, that was all he would give me. He said he had to protect me. I'm so damn tired of being protected, Cam."

"Zach mentioned Hillary Simmons, too. So, he knew... Do you really think that's you?"

She almost didn't explain, but this was Cam. Cam, who had saved her and her father. Cam, who'd done nothing but doggedly follow this whole thing even though it didn't involve him at all. Cam, who *proved* everything her father had ever told her was a lie— from beginning to end.

"Laurel said the name Hillary was on the tape. She said that name and I... It gave me the creeps. Like an icy chill. Like a *ghost*. Why would the name Hillary do that if I wasn't..."

"Okay. Okay." He rubbed her hand between both of his. It was a comfort, an anchor while she was swept away in all these awful, confusing emotions. "Let's try to work this out, piece by piece."

She nodded, even though the thought was exhausting.

"So, we have this group who thinks you're someone else. A name that seems slightly familiar to you. Your father admitting…" He trailed off, his eyes never leaving her face. He cocked his head, his expression falling to something less fierce and more…kind. Sympathetic. "You're dead on your feet, Hilly."

*Hilly. My name isn't even Hilly.* Emotion clogged her throat. "We should go through it," she managed to croak. "We have to figure it out."

With a gentleness that completely undid her, he pulled her shoulders back so she was leaning on him again. He kept his arm around her shoulders, holding her there against the strength of him.

"It'll keep." He brushed his lips against her temple like he had when they'd been hiking. Just a simple expression of comfort, but there'd been so little effortless affection in her life it felt like…everything.

She turned her face into his neck. She

tried really, really hard not to cry. It felt like such a weakness when he was so strong. She could be strong, too. Hadn't she been strong? Hadn't she paid attention? Wasn't she rolling with the punches pretty darn well?

The sob escaped against him, but he didn't even flinch. "Just let it out, baby."

*Baby.* It seemed like that should be insulting somehow, but he said it in such a soft, soothing way it only made her feel good. Safe. Comfortable.

"I don't want to cry," she squeaked, even as tears were tracking down her cheeks. "I want to be strong like you."

"It's pretty easy to be strong when you're not the one who's life has been upended. Besides, crying isn't the absence of strength, Hilly. You can't bottle things like fear and frustration up. That only multiplies them. At some point you have to let them out."

She didn't know how to let it out with someone else around. At least, she thought she didn't. But the tears came easily enough after those words, and it seemed so easy to curl into Cam, to find some solace in the way his hand rubbed up and down her back.

There was such peace in trusting someone with her emotions instead of trying to ignore them or reason them away. Such peace, she woke up sometime later not even realizing she'd fallen asleep on Cam's shoulder.

But he was easing her off now, his weapon drawn.

Sleepy confusion sharpened immediately and she sat straight up.

Cam pointed to the front door. "Someone's out there. It might be Zach, but I want to be careful."

Might be. But he was holding his gun, creeping toward the window. Clearly he had some reservations.

"Go into the bedroom with your father. Just until we're sure."

"Cam."

He turned his attention to her, nodded to the room again. "If it's not Zach, whoever is out there wants you or your father. You need to go wake him up so he's prepared to run if we need to. Okay?"

It was harder than it should have been to choose warning her father over staying with Cam. Except the man inside this bedroom wasn't her father. He'd lied to her for more than twenty years.

And kept her alive.

She squeezed her eyes shut for a second,

blaming the nap and the exhaustion on her brain's circular thinking. She had to focus on one simple thing for the next little while: staying alive.

She might have complicated feelings about the man in the bedroom, but she wanted him alive, too. She slipped into the room, giving Cam one last glance. He stood next to the window, weapon drawn, that look of stoic concentration on his face.

He glanced at her once, clearly waiting for her to get safely in the room before he did anything. If he was only protecting *her*, she would have been furious. Mad that he'd act just like her father trying to *keep* her from things.

But this wasn't only about her. He was also intent on keeping her father safe, and since it seemed they wanted him dead most of all, Hilly had to do her part in keeping Dad safe.

She crept into the room, pulling the door shut behind her. The room was dim, as the world outside the windows was dark. Free had padded toward the door she closed behind her and was now growling low in her throat.

"Dad?"

He wasn't in the bed. He was halfway out the window. She couldn't believe after all

Cam had risked to save them, to help them, Dad was running away.

"What do you think you're doing?" she demanded.

"I'm glad you came back, Hilly. Come on now. We don't have much time."

She could only gape at her father as he slithered out the window and stood outside, holding his arm through the window toward her.

"You have to come with me," he said, as if he was telling her to go do her chores.

She moved toward the window even though she had no intent of going with him. "Go with you where?"

"Away. That man out there wants me dead."

"Who's out there? Is Cam in dan—" Dad lunged and grabbed her arm before she could run back to the door.

"Forget the stranger," Dad said, jerking her toward the window. "We have to save ourselves, Hilly. It's our only chance to survive."

"I can't leave Cam. He saved us. Get back in here. We have to help him. We can't leave him alone. What's wrong with you?"

Dad shook his head, letting go of her arm. "I can't stay. They will kill me, especially that one out there. I don't know why you're trusting a stranger over—"

"Over the man who lied to me my whole entire life?" Hilly demanded.

"No time for that," Dad said flatly. "Make your choice, girl. You've got three seconds."

CAM COULDN'T SEE out the window, but he could hear the careful, patient and quiet attempts to pick the lock.

It wasn't Zach. He'd known that almost right away, but he hadn't wanted to worry Hilly. The most important thing was getting her out of sight, and warning James.

The more they knew, the better. At some point, things would have to make sense and add up. But right now he couldn't figure out who this man was trying to pick the lock.

If it was the Protectors, surely they'd bust in guns blazing with more than one man. Zach had said there were at least thirty in the compound. There was no reason to send one man to pick a lock.

Whoever was out there was huddled close enough to the door Cam couldn't get a glimpse of them through the window.

He debated his two options. Wait for the man to pick the lock and see what would come next, or catch him in the act. Both were a problem because he didn't know if the man was armed, and with what.

So, it was probably better to take him off guard. Letting him open the door himself gave him too much time to plan an attack. Scaring him probably wasn't the best idea, but Cam would be careful.

He listened and waited for the click of the man succeeding in turning the lock, then he acted. He flung the door open before the lock picker could and pointed his gun at the squatting man.

It bothered Cam that the man didn't look all that perturbed, but Cam kept his weapon steady on him.

"Well. Hello." The man slowly dropped the tools he'd used on the door to the ground, then lifted his hands. "Don't shoot," he said with a crooked smile.

Something in his brown eyes made Cam uneasy, but he held the gun trained on the stranger's head. He couldn't take any chances.

The man started to move his hands to the ground.

"Don't move," Cam instructed. He didn't see a weapon, but that didn't mean he couldn't be reaching for one.

"I'm just going to stand up. If that's all right? Bit easier to explain things if I'm not losing the function of my knees being crouched this long."

Since Cam was holding a gun and the man wasn't, Cam inclined his head in assent. Because he was watching the man's hands, making sure they made contact with the ground rather than a grab for a potential weapon, Cam was a second too late to dodge the sweeping kick that knocked him on his side inside the house.

A shooting pain as his hip hit the hard floor had him hissing out a breath. He managed to keep hold of the gun though, trying to get it pointed at the intruder, but a second kick from the man had it flying across the floor.

On a curse, Cam lunged for the weapon, but the man flung himself on top of Cam. Cam fought him off, flipping him easily onto his back and using his body to keep the man on the ground. The man got a cracking elbow blow to Cam's jaw. Stars studded his vision, but Cam landed a blow to the man's side that had the attacker huffing out a pained breath.

Jaw throbbing, Cam grappled with the man, trying to get him subdued. But they rolled, each landing significant blows on the other, and neither really gaining any ground.

Cam didn't dare look at the bedroom door. He could hear Free barking, but he had to hope James and Hilly had the good sense to get out of here in whatever way they could.

Cam managed a decent hold, slowly working his limbs around the strange man and demobilizing both his legs and one arm. He only had to get the other arm locked and—

He saw the glint of a knife with just enough time to react. In a flash, Cam jumped off the man, the blade of the long, vicious knife luckily only catching the gaping fabric of his sweatshirt and nothing else. But the man was on his feet in no time at all, the knife held threateningly in one hand.

Cam didn't let himself obsess over that fact. The most important thing was to stay loose and ready.

"I don't know what you're after, but it isn't me."

The man cocked his head. "You know, you're right, but you have who I'm after, so you'll do for now. Where is he?"

He. This man, who looked to be about the same age as Cam and had clearly had some similar combat training to Cam, wanted James. Not Hilly.

But Cam had made a vow to himself to protect Hilly in whatever way he could. Unfortunately, that meant the vow had to extend to her father.

"I don't know what you're talking about, who you want or why you broke into my cabin."

The man snorted. "Your cabin. What a liar you are. Maybe you're one of *them*."

"Them who?"

"You're a Protector, or should I call you a murderer?" The man lunged with the knife and Cam managed to sidestep. He tried to land a blow, but the man's arm quickly slashed backward, and this time the blade met the flesh of his arm with a sharp sting.

He didn't have time to look at it and discern how deep it was, but it didn't feel too bad.

"I'm not a Protector. I thought you would be."

That seemed to confuse him a little bit and Cam edged farther away from the blade that was now tinged with his blood. If he could back away far enough to be out of lunging distance and look for his gun, he had a chance.

"You're harboring a Protector. That means you're one of them." The stranger took two steps closer for every one Cam managed to edge away.

"I'm not," Cam replied calmly, holding up his hands, trying to make his steps less conspicuous. "I just escaped from them."

"Alone?"

"Yes."

"So that man and woman you came inside with were just figments of my imagination?"

Cam was careful to not let his expression give anything away. "Do you have a lot of figments of imagination?" he asked, his voice even.

"A comedian. Good. Just what my day was miss—"

The front door, which had been partially open from their previous tussle, sprung all the way open. Cam was distracted by the movement, and Zach stepping inside, so it gave the stranger ample opportunity to jump on him and, in a maneuver Cam cursed himself for falling trap to, press the knife's blade to his throat.

Cam looked at Zach, who still stood in the doorway, rifle drawn.

"Shoot him," Cam instructed through gritted teeth, feeling the sharp blade of the knife press harder into his neck. He didn't think this guy was going to wait very much longer to slice him open.

"I can't," Zach returned, slowly lowering his weapon as if he'd somehow been defeated. "He's my brother."

# Chapter Seventeen

Hilly had made her choice, but it wasn't one of the ones Dad had laid out for her. Not that he knew it yet.

There was a kind of giddy freedom in that, no matter the danger they were in. She'd been changed in the past few days, not because she'd found out her father wasn't her own, but because she'd broken out of that stifling prison she hadn't understood and seen the world around her.

It was big and dangerous and scary, but she'd survived. She'd been attacked over and over again and yet she was still running, still fighting. She didn't need her father or even Cam next to her to stand on her own two feet.

From that moment Cam had shown up at her cabin, her life had changed. Opened up. No. That wasn't true. It was the moment she'd decided to leave their clearing, to face the police, to get help.

Even though she'd chickened out, that had gotten the ball rolling. Her choice had changed her life. And for the rest of it, she was going to make the decisions, take the chances and help the people she trusted and loved.

She'd followed Dad away from the cabin in a dead run, and it appeared they hadn't been detected by anyone. It pained her to leave Cam, but she needed Dad away from the danger. Cam had been right that the only person who could be after them at this point was really after her father. She needed to get him to safety.

Cam could hold his own for a while. She had to believe that. But that didn't mean she'd desert him completely.

"Let's take a rest," Hilly said, feigning as much out-of-breath panting as her father was doing.

Even though she now knew the truth about their lack of genetic connections, in her thoughts and feelings he was still her father. She'd have to deal with the complications of that later.

"Shouldn't stop," Dad gasped. "Could be after us."

"I don't think they are. Cam's keeping them

busy. Sit. They'll definitely catch you if you keel over and have a heart attack."

Dad glared, but he didn't argue any further. He found a rock to perch himself on. "I may not be your father by blood, but I've been your father for twenty years and I've always called the shots."

"Well, that all changed when you abandoned me and I realized how helpless you'd left me."

"Helpless! You knew how to hunt and cook and protect yourself. What more would you need?" Dad blustered. The defensiveness he always relied upon when they disagreed was different now—whether because of the position they were in or because she'd simply opened her eyes in this manner, too.

His defensiveness didn't come from a place of rightness. It came from a place of fear. Fear *she* was right.

Which she was, and she was done stuffing down her own truth for his comfort. "I could have used the knowledge of where I could go to get supplies," she shot back. "Any clue as to what the outside world was like so I could navigate it. You left me *helpless* and scared. I was worried sick about you."

"You should have trusted me," he grumbled.

She threw her hands up in the air. It wasn't

the time for this argument, but he made her so angry the words just poured out. "I thought you were dead or hurt. I knew I had to find you and save you, but you left me helpless. I had to find someone to help me because I had none of the skills necessary to save you if it was even possible."

"You shouldn't have ever gone to the outside. And you shouldn't even think about contacting that stranger again. You can't trust—"

"I trust Cam with my life. And yours," she said vehemently, and it was the reminder of Cam that made her rein in her temper and focus on getting back to him. He probably didn't need her help, but that didn't mean she wouldn't offer it.

"I taught you better—"

"We don't have time for this. I need to know everything you know." Then she'd run back to Cam armed with the information she needed.

"That isn't necessary."

She looked into her father's eyes—the man she'd believed to be her father for twenty years. He *had* protected her, and she realized he must have sacrificed for that protection. "Dad, you have to tell me. If you can't tell me, then these past twenty years were for nothing."

He looked away, stubbornly clenching his jaw together.

A tear escaped her eye, but she brushed it away. She'd run back to Cam now. Help him in whatever way she could, even if it wasn't with information.

"They'd found out about you," Dad said, his voice low and pained, causing her to pause her escape plans. "I don't know how. I thought I was just going to our annual meeting, but they tied me up and knocked me around and demanded to know where you were. I wouldn't tell them, but I wasn't the only one looking for you."

"What?"

"Your biological family. Your body was never found back then, and some of them were sure that meant you were still alive."

"Why were you supposed to kill me?" she managed to whisper.

"Revenge." He sighed, rubbing a hand over his chest and making her worry about her heart-attack crack. "Your biological father led the ATF raid that ended with twenty of our men killed. We couldn't let that stand."

Her body went cold. "You were going to kill an innocent *baby* for revenge?"

"You don't know what your father took from us," Dad snapped, eyes blazing with fury time had certainly not calmed. "Twenty men *and* women. All ours. All just trying to make the world a better place."

"Yes, I felt firsthand how your group of associates is trying to make the world a better place."

Dad shook his head. "You can't understand. You won't."

"Why…" She swallowed. "Why didn't you kill me then?"

Dad looked down at his hands. "You were just a tiny thing," he said, all that fury draining out of him. "We'd caused a car accident. It was supposed to be one of the boys, but only you and your father were in the car. I took you out of the car seat and you smiled at me."

"My…father?"

"It wasn't supposed to be a bad accident. We didn't want *him* dead. The point had been to kill one of his children so he'd understand what he'd done. So he'd pay for what he'd done. But part of the guardrail he hit broke off and killed him instantly."

"Killed him," Hilly echoed.

"It seemed silly to kill you, too. The man we wanted revenge on was dead. But my superiors still wanted you dead and I just… I couldn't. I made up a story about being made by the cops so I had to go hide out in Idaho for a while, but after a year they wanted me back in the fold. When we lived in Idaho, I left you with a neighbor who just thought I was a hapless single father. When you were old enough to be on your own, we moved to the cabin. I knew I could keep you safe and out of sight there and no one would come snooping for you—your family or the Protectors. And it worked. All these years it worked."

All these years. Her life had been a lie *all these years*. She wanted to curl up in a ball and cry, but Cam was out there protecting her and her... No, she wasn't sure she could think of this man as her father anymore. He'd killed a man, accidentally or not, out of revenge. Yes, he'd saved her, but...not really.

"So, who burned down the cabin?" she asked through her tight throat. "You said it wasn't the Protectors."

"Your brother. Before you cast stones on our revenge, you might consider your brother has been trying to enact some for years."

"Brother." She had a brother. Looking for her. Wanting to avenge their father's wrongful death. Hilly had to force herself to breathe. So much anger and violence she was in the middle of and she couldn't even wrap her mind around it.

"He's after me. Has been for a few years now. He wasn't close until the past few months, though."

"Is that who's there? My brother is back at the cabin with Cam?"

"Yes, but—"

Two people—both without the full story—facing off in an isolated cabin. It was a recipe for disaster, and she couldn't let it happen.

CAM HAD SURVIVED a lot of tight spots in his day, but a knife to the throat was a new one. Especially while a brotherly yelling match went on around him, with Free's incessant barking and clawing from behind the bedroom door seemingly unnoticed by the bickering siblings.

Cam could feel the slow roll of blood down his neck before it soaked into the collar of his shirt. Nothing fatal, but not particularly comfortable when the blade was still settled there against his skin.

"Ethan," Zach said, sounding tired. "I can't get you out of this if you don't stop. Here and now." He was calm, even if they were arguing, but there was a kind of resigned finality to the way he spoke with his brother that had Cam reconsidering risking a deeper cut with a well-timed elbow or punch.

"Get me out of it," the brother yelled, right in Cam's ear. "Get me out of it? When will you understand there is no *out*? There's only revenge."

"Then what?" Zach demanded, temper straining. "What happens after revenge? You rot in jail."

"Perhaps you two could have this conversation without a knife pressed to my throat?" Cam offered, not thinking the brother would actually release him. Still, it was worth a shot to remind the two he was still here and in the middle of whatever thing they were arguing about.

"He doesn't know anything, Ethan. Let the man go."

Cam winced as the knife only settled deeper into the cut.

"He liberated James before I could," Ethan shot back, tightening his hold. "He knows something."

"Who the hell do you think is *with* James? Can't you see who he's really protecting?"

"It doesn't matter," Ethan said stubbornly.

Cam considered his angles. Drop to the floor and risk the knife cutting vital organs. A jerk to the right and he risked being stabbed just about anywhere. If he thought the man was dead set on killing him, those two moves would be preferable, but Cam still had hope this ended with Ethan letting him go of his own accord. Whatever they were arguing about, whatever Ethan thought, Cam figured it was clear Ethan needed some psychiatric help.

"If this is revenge, how does she not matter?" Zach asked, pinching the bridge of his nose.

"It's revenge for *Dad*. She..." Ethan trailed off, his grip on Cam loosening. "Revenge for Dad is the important thing."

Cam tried to piece that together. Hilly was the she, but Cam couldn't figure out how on earth she fit into plans of revenge or these two disparate brothers.

"Mom won't think so," Zach said quietly.

"She should!" Ethan shot back, the volume of Ethan's voice in Cam's ear making him flinch and then hiss out a breath as the knife cut more skin.

He was done. Risking further damage, Cam feigned a cough and then used Ethan's slight pull away as the opportunity to strike an elbow to Ethan's neck. It didn't dislodge the knife from his hand, but it did give Cam the space of seconds to escape the hold without making his cut too much worse.

But Ethan immediately lunged, tackling

him at an awkward side angle. Cam saw the flash of the knife and managed to roll away from the first downward strike, but Ethan was on top of him quickly.

Cam grabbed his wrists, holding the sharp point of the knife away, but Ethan being on top gave him the better angle with which to force the blade down. Cam tried to kick or struggle, but most of his strength was focused on holding off the blade.

Cam took a chance at looking around the room, trying to figure out where the hell Zach was, but then he saw him. At the door, trying to push Hilly back out.

Straining to hold off the increasing force of Ethan's push, Cam gritted his teeth. "Run, Hilly," he ordered.

He couldn't hear what they were saying, or see if Hilly listened to him or Zach got her out of here. The knife was inching closer and closer to the vulnerable flesh of his neck. Ethan's eyes glittered with malice and hate.

Then Hilly appeared in his vision with Zach's rifle in her hand. She skittered behind Ethan and shoved the barrel into his back. Her eyes were wild and her breath was coming in pants. "Get off of him, now," she ordered.

Ethan looked down at Cam. Everything in his gaze was cold, dead almost. It gave Cam

a full-body chill. For a second, he truly believed he would make Hilly take the shot.

"I'm your sister," Hilly said breathlessly. "I
don't want to hurt you, but I will if you don't
stop this right now."

After a moment of continued struggle,
Ethan began to ease off. He didn't let go of
the knife, but he began to move it away from
Cam's throat as he slid into a crouch. Cam
kept a hold on Ethan's wrists anyway. He
wasn't about to believe even with a gun on
him Ethan would give up easily.

Cam surreptitiously tried to move his legs
so he could keep Ethan from making any sudden moves, but that only made Ethan laugh.
In the midst of that laughter that seemed to
startle everyone, he twisted and grabbed the
barrel of the weapon, jerking it out of Hilly's
grasp.

Cam moved to his feet, but he ended up
only getting into a sitting position before he
broke Hilly's fall. She crashed into him hard,
and he fell backward a little, but he quickly
maneuvered to position himself between
Hilly and Ethan.

Ethan stood there, Zach's rifle secure in
his hands, pointing it right at Cam. Hilly was
struggling behind him, but Cam wasn't about
to let her in front of him.

"Ethan," Zach said, breathless horror in his voice. "You're not going to shoot your own siblings."

Zach moved, but Ethan trained the sight right on Zach's chest, making Zach freeze.

Ethan jabbed the gun toward him and then Cam. "I could kill all three of you and frame James. His prints are in here. He could finally pay for what he did to my father."

"Please," Hilly whispered, getting to her feet. "Don't make this worse."

"It's already worse!" Ethan screamed.

Cam jumped to his feet. Without having to say anything, Zach inched closer so they created a barricade between Hilly and Ethan. Ethan ordered them to stop, but Cam wouldn't. "I won't let you kill your own sister, Ethan. Not if I can help it."

"You can't," Ethan said, the gun trained on Cam. He put his finger on the trigger and Cam sucked in a breath.

Hilly pushed at him and Zach, but Cam would be damned if he moved. He'd take a bullet for her ten times over. He'd tackle Ethan before he shot, then Zach would have a chance of getting Hilly out of here.

But another voice joined Hilly's protests. There were footsteps from behind them, then James came into view. He looked grim and determined, red-faced and panting, but calm nevertheless.

"You want to kill someone, you kill the man you're really after," James said gruffly.

Ethan's gaze sharpened, and the gun's barrel moved with swift accuracy to James's chest.

Cam didn't think, didn't even breathe. He lunged.

# Chapter Eighteen

"No." Hilly wasn't sure if she only thought it or if she screamed it, but the red splotch that bloomed on Cam's thigh and his subsequent crash to the ground had her swaying on her feet. Then rushing forward, trying and failing to soften his fall.

He cursed under his breath, writhing in pain as he grabbed at his leg. "Would someone get all his weapons," Cam said through gritted teeth, his body shivering. "I'm a little done with being his punching bag."

Hilly shook, but she focused on what she had to do. Zach—the man who'd led them around the decoy camp—was taking care of Ethan, and whatever fight they were having Hilly couldn't pay attention to. She couldn't think about how he was her brother, how he was mixed up in this. How her other brother wanted her dad dead. Cam was shot. *Shot.*

She looked up at her dad—she wished she

could think of him as James, as a stranger, but he was her father. Secrets didn't erase twenty plus years. "We need bandages."

Dad shrugged. "Leave him. It'd be the best thing for everyone if we just leave him."

Hilly gaped at the man she'd called father. "He saved you," she seethed. "You will do everything in your power to help him or I will shoot you myself."

Dad's jaw went hard, and he didn't move. Hilly felt tears filling her eyes, but she blinked them away.

"Fine. I'll do it myself. Bandages. I can find bandages. You stay put."

"S-stop the bleeding," Cam said, the shivering getting even worse as he cursed. "You need to stop it, Hilly."

She swallowed and nodded. She made a move to unzip her coat, but Dad finally stirred, crouching next to Cam's leg. He pushed a bundle of fabric onto the red seeping wound. "Press this hard. Even if it hurts. Harder you press, less blood."

Even though her hands shook, she did as Dad said, pressing the fabric onto the wound. Cam hissed out a breath, but he didn't tell her to stop.

"We need to get him help," Hilly said.

"This is bad." She gently touched his neck underneath the nasty-looking gash.

"Survived worse," Cam gritted out.

"When?"

"Okay, maybe not worse exactly..."

Hilly looked over at Zach and Ethan. Her brothers, apparently. It appeared as if Zach had won the fight. He was now tying Ethan to a chair. She hoped to God it was tight enough to keep him there. Regardless of their genetic connection, the man was not in his right mind. Not to be trusted.

"Dad," she whispered. "We need help."

Dad sighed heavily, but then he did something that had her jaw dropping. He pulled a phone out of his pocket. A slim device just like the one Cam had that had been left in his pack. Dad had a phone. A *phone*.

It struck her as deeply unfair and symbolic of everything that had been stolen from her, and she didn't even have time to be upset over it because Cam had been *shot*.

He spoke into the phone. "We have a man who's been shot, and the shooter waylaid. We're at an isolated cabin and—"

"Tell them to meet me at mile marker 32 on Highway A," Zach instructed.

Hilly looked up at him. He was grim and pale. She glanced back to Ethan, who was now secured to the chair, his lip split and bleeding, fury and pure hate in his gaze.

Hilly looked back at Zach. Both of them her brothers, and yet she couldn't dwell on that. "How are you going to get him there?"

"I can fit him in the back of my four-wheeler and drive him down to that spot, but I can only fit him and one other person to make sure he's not bouncing around too much back there. Still, better to be quick about it. I can get down there faster than I can instruct an ambulance up here."

"I'll go with you."

Zach shook his head sadly. "I'm sorry. I can't trust James with my brother. James will need to go with the police."

"Police? Who cares about James and police? Get Cam to a hospital!" How could these men stand around acting like their vendettas were the most important thing when Cam, who had no connection to any of this, was in pain and his life was in danger? What was wrong with them?

"I will. I *am*, but I have to take James in, too."

"What about him?" she demanded, jabbing a hand at Ethan.

Zach sighed. "He'll face the law, as well.

I'll send an officer back to take care of him, and get you."

Hilly didn't realize she was shaking her head no until Zach crouched next to her. Gently and carefully he placed a hand on her shoulder. "I know this is a mess. I'm sorry for that. But I need you to stay here with him. I can't trust James with my—*our* brother."

"He *shot* Cam."

"I know. I know. He'll be arrested. I promise you that. I won't stand in the way of the law after the lengths he's gone to to thwart it, but that doesn't make him not my brother. It doesn't make me not love him."

Hilly swallowed at the lump in her throat. These men were all working with competing interests, so self-absorbed in their own crap. Well, she wouldn't let Cam pay the price for that.

She kept pressing on the wound, but fixed Zach with the best intimidating look she could muster. "Go get the vehicle," she ordered. "Bring it as close to the door as you can. Dad, you go get a blanket off the bed. Something we can make a kind of stretcher out of and—"

"I can get up," Cam said on a gasp of pain.

"Don't you dare try," Hilly snapped. "Once

we've got that, find any pillows or soft things we can put down in the back to make him comfortable."

Both her father and Zach looked at her with furrowed brows. "Now!" she yelled, and they hopped to it.

"Drill Sergeant Hilly," Cam murmured. His eyes were fluttering closed and his breathing was too shallow for her to have any kind of comfort.

She pushed harder on the wound and his eyes flew open on a yelp of pain.

"You stay conscious, you hear me?"

"Yes, ma'am," he said, the corners of his mouth somehow curving upward. "Might have just fallen in love with you right here. But it might also be the blood loss talking."

Hilly thought her heart might have stopped, but she wasn't about to let him know. "Well, you better make it through this so you can decide if it's real or the blood loss."

His hand brushed her arm. "Real enough, I'd think."

"Then you really better survive," she said, fighting back the tears. "So far you've only managed to give me my first kiss. Going to need a first date out of you, too."

"Correction. Not drill sergeant. General Hilly."

"I'll take it," she replied.

Dad returned with the blankets and some pillows, and when Zach came back, they all worked to get Cam loaded up. She wanted to cry. She wanted to tell him she loved him, but she was afraid it would feel too much like a goodbye.

Once Cam was settled, she wrapped her arms around him. She brushed her mouth against his. "Fight, Cam. I know you can."

He managed a weak, lethargic salute.

Zach handed her his rifle, and Cam's handgun. "Make sure Ethan stays tied up." Zach took a deep breath in, and then let it out on a sigh. "I'm trusting you, Hillary."

She didn't correct her name. Instead she held his gaze and nodded at Cam. "Same goes."

Zach nodded. He gave her arm a squeeze before climbing into the driver's seat. Dad sat stiffly next to Cam, and yet Hilly knew he'd keep him stable. For her.

Hilly couldn't watch them drive away because every bump made her wince in sympathy pain for what Cam must be going through.

She turned to the cabin and stepped back inside. Ethan was sitting in the chair. The bonds looked uncomfortable. She hoped they *hurt* for what he'd done to Cam. She walked over to the bedroom door, then opened it.

Free leaped out, whimpering and jumping at her. She soothed the dog with words, and once she'd set down the handgun, with pats.

"I hope he dies," Ethan said coldly.

Hilly murmured the stay command into Free's ear, giving her a kiss on her soft fur. Slowly, she stood. Slowly, she took stock of this man who was supposed to be her brother.

"So you can be a murderer?" She kept the acid out of her tone, the fury. She looked at him and held his vicious gaze.

*Might have just fallen in love with you right here.* Cam had said those words to her. Maybe losing consciousness and in incredible pain, but he'd said that to her. Cam wouldn't say that frivolously. He'd mean it.

Was that what she felt? Did she even *know* what she felt? A sheltered girl in the midst of some kind of messed-up situation she couldn't even begin to explain.

Then there was this man, spouting his anger and his hate, and any sympathy she might have had for him had died when he shot Cam.

"A murderer," Ethan said, his voice sounding so *pleasant* it sent a shudder through her. "Just like the man you seem to think is your father. He's the murderer. He's the evil. I'm balancing the scales. Making everything right. I should have killed him. I *would* have. Any man who tries to save him deserves to die, too."

The idea that Cam deserved to die made her so furious, she crossed to the man who was supposedly her brother. She slapped him as hard as she could, her palm stinging enough to bring tears to her eyes. "You're just as bad as them. The Protectors and their revenge."

He jerked in his chair, trying to pull his limbs free, but Zach had done a fine job of tying him down. "You were raised by one of them. What does that make you?"

"I've never tried to kill anyone. Never let revenge cloud reason. Look what you've done. Hurt everyone around you, and for what?"

"He killed our father."

"He didn't mean to." She knew it was a weak excuse, and if she'd known her biological father instead of James as her father maybe she'd feel like Ethan did. "I know that doesn't solve anything. I know it doesn't heal anything for you. He was doing something wrong, and our father paid a price no one should have to pay, but you can't bring him back, Ethan."

"But I can cause the man who killed him irreparable pain and suffering."

"At the sake of losing out on everything? We're awfully different, Ethan." He winced when she said his name, so she kept using it. "I don't know who I would have been if things had been different. But I have been sheltered and hidden away for twenty years, and even when you don't realize it, it's a kind of prison. It stifles you. Trust me, Ethan, you don't want that for the rest of your life. There are things you're going to want to experience outside of revenge."

Things like love. Regardless of whether she *should* or not. Whether it made sense or not. It was very clear to her after this whole unraveling of who she truly was that life very, very rarely made sense.

"Revenge is all I want," Ethan said vehemently.

"Then I just feel sad for you, Ethan." It was true. The anger melted away until she had only pity for this warped man who didn't even want the good things out of life.

She did. All of them she could get. Regardless of who she was or who she loved. She wanted to experience it all.

HILLY WASN'T SURE how long it was before two police officers showed up. She'd hoped Laurel would be one of them so she could feel somewhat at ease, but then again Laurel was probably with Cam. Her brother. Her wounded brother.

The men arrested Ethan in short order. She was asked a plethora of questions before she was led to a police cruiser. Hilly was ushered into the passenger seat in the front. She insisted Free sit on her lap, and was indulged after a short argument.

The second officer and Ethan sat in the back. The ride to town was long and quiet except for the occasional burst of police radio activity.

They wouldn't give her any information on Cam's prognosis, but they had agreed to drop her off at the hospital. The ride felt interminable, but eventually the cruiser pulled up in front of a gray building that made Hilly's stomach cramp with fear.

She didn't know how to navigate hospitals or the outside world or any of this, but still the door was being opened for her and she was being asked to step out.

There was an odd pang at leaving Ethan handcuffed and alone with these quiet, serious-faced police officers. He was her brother, and maybe what he really needed was love and hope.

But when she got out of the cruiser, Zach

was there. He held up his hand to her, asking her to wait, while he spoke in low tones with the driver of the police vehicle. At one point he even flashed a badge.

He came back to her side of the car and failed in his clear attempt at a smile.

"Are you with the police?" she asked, wondering about the badge, his role with the Protectors, trying to work it all out.

"FBI," Zach said sheepishly. "Well, I went a little rogue, so it's possible I'm no longer FBI once I turn myself in, but I was undercover with the Protectors to build a case against them."

"Did I ruin it?"

He reached out, hesitated and then touched her shoulder gently. "You didn't ruin anything, Hilly. Not by a long shot."

"Can I… Could we…"

He blinked, but then he seemed to understand, and slowly, carefully and awkwardly on both their parts, they shared a quick hug.

"I'm going to go with Ethan. Um, listen, I called my…our mother. I told her to stay put, but she's not much on taking orders from me. It's possible she shows up here. She's going to…" He swallowed. "This will be an awful big deal for her. She doesn't live too far away.

So, I might not be able to get back in time to…facilitate."

"Go with Ethan. He needs someone. I can handle…" Her mother. Mother.

It hadn't even occurred to her, that there would be more. She had a mother. Her skin felt too tight at the very idea of one.

She had a mother.

And this brother in front of her. She looked up at him, trying to focus on one emotion at a time. "Can you do me one favor?"

"Anything."

Hilly looked down at Free. "I don't have a house. I don't have anyone but Cam. I—"

"I'll figure out a place for her till you're settled. Sound good?"

She nodded.

Zach gave Free a pat, but he spoke as he did it. "I hope you understand that he's sick, Hilly." There was a depth of grief in his voice Hilly had never really known. "He needs help. Real help."

She nodded. Clearly Zach still had hope for his—*their* brother, and she didn't want to dull any of that hope for him.

Zach got in the car with Free, and the cruiser drove away, leaving Hilly completely and utterly alone in a brand-new world.

Before, it might have scared her, might

have rendered her completely paralyzed, but she had done so much in these past few days. Somewhere in this building Cam was possibly fighting for his life and she needed to be there.

She marched in the front doors. There was a big airy lobby, people walking this way and that. There was a directory on the wall, a bunch of different medical words ending in *ology*.

Emergency. Cam would be in Emergency.

She started to move toward it, but a commotion behind her had her looking back. Laurel rushed inside, her hair wild, and she wasn't in her uniform. There was a big, burly bearded man with her.

"Hilly. God." She crossed to her and grabbed her hands. "How is he? Where is he? What happened? Did—"

"Ease up, princess," the man murmured. "One question at a time."

"I just got here," Hilly managed, incapable of looking away from the wild-looking man with Laurel. "I don't know anything."

"All right. Let's head to Emergency, then," the man said authoritatively.

Hilly shied away, but her hands were still clutched in Laurel's. Laurel looked at her, then back at the man with her, before squeezing and releasing Hilly's hands.

"This is Grady. My fiancée."

Hilly's jaw went a little slack. She supposed you couldn't judge people based on appearances, but Grady looked like he could be some kind of outlaw from the Wild West, while even with her disheveled hair Laurel looked prim and proper.

"See, even strangers can't believe we're getting married," Grady said with a kind smile, and then he was leading them toward Emergency like he knew where to go. They stepped into a waiting area and Laurel marched right up to the woman behind the counter.

"Why don't you sit?" Grady said, pointing to a chair. "The way I hear it, you've been through the wringer."

The way he heard it. He'd heard things. Hilly felt dizzy, so she sat. Laurel marched back over, looking grim.

"All they can tell me is he's in surgery. Dad's trying to get a flight out of Denver, Jen is closing up the store and Dylan's on his way." Laurel was all jangling nervousness, as if she'd absorbed all the energy that had leaked out of Hilly.

"What happened? The cops told me some, but… I don't understand."

"I'm not sure *I* understand," Hilly replied.

Laurel took her hand again, sliding into the chair next to her. "Finding out you aren't who you thought can't be easy on top of all this. They told me they've arrested your father. Once we find out about Cam, I can take you down to the jail, if you'd like."

"That's…so kind."

"Cam cares for you. That was obvious. So, while he's getting all stitched up, we'll take care of each other, okay?"

Hilly wanted to cry. People who wanted not just to take care of her or protect her, but be cared for and protected in return. It was a miracle in the midst of all this confusion and fear.

"Lewis?"

They all looked up at a slim brunette woman with large eyes who'd approached Grady.

"No, I'm sorry. Lewis was my father," Grady said, brows furrowed. "Lewis Carson. Did you know him?"

"Oh, of course. You're…too young. It's just been…" She pressed a hand to her temple, clearly out of sorts and upset. "You're his son. He has a son."

"Ma'am, I—"

"My name's Sarah."

Grady's face went slack. "Sarah. Sarah, my dad's sister who ran away?"

She smiled sadly and nodded. "Yes. That would be me. I can't believe... God, it's a day for family reunions and I..." She shook her head, curling her hands into fists. "One thing at a time," she muttered.

Something was buzzing along Hilly's skin. Prickly and uncomfortable, and part of her wanted to back away, but she couldn't stop staring at the woman talking to Grady.

"I so want to catch up, but I'm here looking for..." The woman's eyes met hers, and there was a brief moment where they both didn't breathe.

Hilly hadn't noticed any glaring similarities between herself and Ethan and Zach, but this woman... It was like looking into a slightly warped mirror. Same eyes, nose and mouth. Their hair color was different, but the eyes...

"Hillary," the woman breathed.

"I..." She didn't know what to say, and even the "I" came out like a squeak.

"Zach said you'd be here. I... He told me not to come. I shouldn't have come. I had to come." She reached out, then snatched her hands back.

Something about seeing this woman so nervous, tears flowing, smoothed all that over in Hilly. She stood without shaking at all and smiled at the woman.

Her mother.

"I'm glad you're here."

The woman choked on a sob, so Hilly held open her arms. She knew it would take time to truly work through all this. To figure out how a mother-daughter relationship worked after twenty years of not knowing or thinking the other still lived, but Hilly now figured the best way to start anything was with open arms and an open heart.

The woman hugged her and sobbed into her shoulder. Hilly cried a little, too, but she didn't fall apart. She felt so…strong. So sure. There were still so many question marks in her life, but now she knew who she was.

Now she could begin.

"I thought you were dead," the woman sobbed. "I mourned you, grieved you and your father, and here you are."

She let the woman cry on her shoulder, held her and soothed her. "Here I am," she whispered.

Slowly the woman pulled herself together,

pulled away. "God. What a day. One son's in jail, my daughter's back from the dead. My nephew..." She turned to Grady. "I... I can't..."

"Sit," Laurel urged, pointing to the seat Hilly had vacated. "Let's all take a minute to breathe and then talk."

That was just what they did. Sarah explained how when her father didn't approve of her marrying a man in law enforcement, she ran away, cutting herself completely off from the family. She talked about Hilly's biological father's work with the ATF. Hilly explained a little bit about her growing up, though glossed over some things left for a better time.

None of them talked about Cam, even as Jen and Dylan joined them, as if in tacit agreement, but Hilly's mind was never far from him.

When a nurse called Laurel's name, she was allowed to go back. Since Hilly wasn't family, she had to stay in the waiting room. All the siblings took turns going in, and Hilly looked longingly after each one.

But they assured her he was stable, just not conscious. When Cam's father arrived and was brought up to speed, he sat on the opposite side of the room as Sarah.

Laurel sighed. "I can't believe he could think of the feud at a time like this."

"Feud?" Hilly asked.

"Carsons and Delaneys," Sarah replied, holding her hand. She smiled fondly at Grady. "So, Bent hasn't changed?"

"Not a bit."

"Except for a Carson and Delaney getting married in a month," Laurel returned.

Grady grinned. "Oh, right, except for that." He turned his grin to Hilly, before looking back at Laurel. "Can I be in the room when you tell your brother his woman is a Carson?"

A Carson. Family feuds. *Family.* It was overwhelming, but somehow as long as Cam was okay, and her father was okay… Hilly figured it'd be amazing.

## Chapter Nineteen

Cam was sure his head had been stuffed with cotton, and maybe his blood had been replaced with lava. But he was somehow packed in ice. Needles made of ice.

He was in hell.

He struggled to swim his way out of it. If he could just open his eyes, maybe this would all go away. It seemed as though it took forever before he managed the Herculean feat.

Laurel's face wavered in his vision. It was a comfort his sister was here. Wherever he was. She wasn't crying, so he figured that was good, but one never could be sure about these things. "Did I die?"

"Not yet," she returned. She was trying to sound brave, but her voice was scratchy.

"That's good, I guess."

"We're going to have to stop meeting like this, big brother."

Hospital. He was in a hospital. Because

he'd been shot somewhere along the line. Was that why his leg throbbed worse than the rest of his body? It hurt too much to try to piece it all together. "Mine's worse," Cam managed. Laurel had been hurt last year, right when he'd come home to Bent. While he wasn't big on winning this competition, he hoped it would smooth some of the jagged worry edges off her expression.

"Where's Hilly?" he asked. Because Hilly didn't have anywhere to go. He'd left her in that cabin, and where would she be? Who would take care of her?

"She's here. Dad, Jen, Dylan. Everyone is here waiting for you to wake up. We had to take turns watching you sleep."

"Someone should take care of her. She's been through so much. Been braver than anyone has a right to be. She's got to be exhausted. What time is it? What— She doesn't have anywhere to go."

"Shh." Laurel touched his cheek, a rare affectionate gesture that would normally make him uncomfortable, but right now it felt good to have someone he loved touch him gently. "Hilly's mother and Zach are both here and watching after her, but we couldn't tear that woman away with a herd of wild horses. She's not going until she sees you."

"Her mother. She met her mother?"

"They seemed to be getting along pretty well. Hilly's holding up like a champ for all she's been through."

"I need to see her."

"She wants to see you, but they're saying family only."

"Laurel."

Her mouth curved. "I'll have Grady create a diversion and sneak her back."

He breathed out, relief coursing through him.

"Carsons come in handy. You might want to keep that in mind," she said cryptically. Then she sighed. "Ten years in the Marines and no matter how I worried, you never got hurt. You're home for less than a year and look at all the trouble you've gotten yourself into."

"I guess Bent does that to a person."

She smiled, as he'd hoped she would, but here in this groggy space of not being totally with it, he felt the emotion of all he'd been through crash through him, breaking down walls he didn't know he'd erected. "I failed. There. Here."

She brushed a kiss across his forehead. It comforted him somehow. "You know, I've felt that way a time or two in my career, but

Grady tends to remind me I did the best I could with what I had. I know you're probably thinking there are a million different scenarios that would have had a better outcome, but you don't know that. One thing you know and I know is you gave it your all. You always have. It's not a failure if we're doing that. It can't be."

Maybe it was all the medication softening his brain, but that soothed his conscience in a lot of ways.

"We'll get Hilly back in a few. Stay awake." She patted his shoulder and then left the room.

Cam lay there, mostly because he didn't have a choice, but Laurel's words stuck with him. He had always done the best he could. It was hard to know his best was sometimes just not enough, but Hilly was safe. She'd found her father *and* her family.

He felt like a failure because he hadn't been the one to tie up all the loose ends, but did it matter when he'd given everything he could to keep her and her father safe? His friendship hadn't been enough to save Aaron, but he would have done the same for Aaron. He just hadn't had the chance.

Maybe it was time to stop beating himself up for not having the chance.

The door squeaked open and Hilly slid in. She didn't hesitate, didn't seem taken aback by the machines hooked up to him. She walked right over and, with some care to the IV and his injuries, laid her head against his chest.

"Oh, Cam. You're okay."

"Okay," he agreed. Better with her here. He didn't know how a person could fill up your life in such a short time, but the thought of her not in his about did him in.

Hilly looked up, tears filling her eyes. "Laurel said you'll need another surgery."

"I'll live. Survived the first one, didn't I?"

A tear slipped out and he reached over with his non-IV arm to brush it away. "You know, you didn't cry the whole time in that cabin when your brothers were there. You kept it all together while they fought, while I fought."

"I wanted to be strong for you." She touched the bandage on his neck, her fingertips like heaven against his skin. He wanted to grab her wrist and hold her hand there forever, but she pulled away before his brain could get the messaging to his limbs.

"I heard you met your mother."

Hilly nodded. "It's very strange. But she's nice. Easy to talk to in a way. She doesn't expect too much. It's…"

"Weird?"

"Very weird. But I kind of have to start my life over, so I figure it'd be weird no matter what. My… James and Ethan were both arrested. Zach seemed hopeful that Ethan would get recommended to psychiatric care, and because James hadn't meant to kill my father, and because he's actually been a model citizen since, his sentence wouldn't be too harsh. If he pleads guilty. Laurel said she'd take me to see him, but—"

"You take her up on that, okay? You take any Delaney up on anything they offer. You hear me?" His mouth quirked. "You said that to me. Told me to stay awake. You were very forceful."

She slid her hand into his and smiled. "Well, I am pretty tough."

He lifted her hand to his mouth, but couldn't quite work out the strength to actually brush a kiss over it. "The toughest."

"Apparently I'm a Carson."

Cam laughed, though it hurt. "Let me guess. Grady put you up to that. Though I think he'd want to be here to watch my reaction."

Hilly looked at him so seriously. "No. It's true. My mother is Grady's aunt—I guess she ran away from Bent and the Carsons to marry my father. She recognized him right away. I can see why. It's hard to believe I'm related to someone that…whatever he is."

The cottony feeling in his head returned, but with an extra dose of a buzzing sound. She was serious. She was a… Carson. A Carson. The family he'd spent his whole life looking down his nose at, and maybe that had eased some since he'd been back and Grady and his cousins had proved indispensable in saving Laurel from her kidnapping last year, but… A Carson.

"He wanted to be here when you were told," Hilly said, her eyebrows furrowed together. "I guess I understand why."

"I… You're…" Surely he was hallucinating.

She cocked her head. "Do my blood relations change the way you feel about me, Cam? You told me you loved me."

"Did I?" he muttered, shifting uncomfortably in bed. Not because of the Carson thing, but because he'd said a lot of things after he'd been shot that he wouldn't have said in his right mind. He would have waited. He would have…set the stage. Not confessed his feelings when he'd been not totally convinced he was going to live.

It didn't change the feelings. They were there, but no matter how strong she was, how amazing she was, she had a new life to build. A million things to figure out. She didn't need him muddying things up while she was trying to figure out a brand-new family, and to reconcile what James had done with the man who'd taken care of her as a father for twenty years.

"Must have been the gunshot wound," he offered, trying to ease away from the conversation. Giving her an out, some space, but she only frowned at him.

He swallowed, nerves battling it out with the desperate need to just... She was everything he wanted. He'd been around enough to know she was different and special. That love didn't knock you sideways out of the blue with just anyone. "That was a joke."

"Are you sure?" she asked, so serious, so...

Hell. "I do love you, Hilly. There's a rational part of my brain that says it's too much too soon, but it doesn't erase the feeling. You have so much ahead of you. A new life. You have more important things—"

"More important things? You are an important thing. You're at the center of this new life because it's here because of you. You gave me protection, Cam, but you also gave me choices. I know there's a lot out there I don't know, but..." She looked at their linked hands, working through it all. Always so determined to do just that.

"My mother," she said carefully, "and my brother love me. They don't know me, but I'm theirs, so, they love me. I feel it. I don't know how to love them back yet, but I'll learn. Why would I run away from the learning?"

"You wouldn't," Cam said. "You're too brave."

Her mouth curved. "Then I'm brave enough to handle that, and figure out what my future holds, and know that I want you in it. I don't need to understand the world to understand that, to understand you."

Cam cleared his throat, trying to get past the emotion clogged there. "You might find that someone else would come along and be more—"

"They wouldn't be you. I don't need a million men lined up for me to make my choice. I just need the best." With her free hand she reached out and cupped his face. "I don't know a lot of men, but I know you'll always be among the best I know. You cared about me when you didn't have to. You wanted to make things right because they should be. You gave me a choice when I'd never had one before. So, here's my choice. I choose you. I love you."

It humbled him. Her strength. That she could put her feelings into words like that. "I don't have the words…"

"That's okay. I'll give you a few days after you've been shot to find them."

He chuckled. "I guess we should work on that first date," he said, his voice coming out raspy at best.

"You'll need to lose this." She tapped the IV.

"I'll get there."

She rested her head on his chest again. "God, I'm tired."

"Rest. We'll both rest. Together." Because he was determined to make *together* work, no matter what came their way.

# *Epilogue*

*One month later*

Hilly looked at the little cabin on Delaney property. For the past month of building her life, she hadn't been able to be shy about accepting help. When you had nothing, you had to accept other people giving you something.

Now she had a cabin that had once been Laurel's. She had two part-time jobs—waitressing some nights at Grady's saloon, Rightful Claim, and cashiering at Jen's general store during the day. And her arms were full of college applications.

She stepped into the cabin, grinning to herself.

Over the past few weeks, Sarah had helped her with the paperwork and proving she'd done the homeschooling work of a high school diploma with James. She knew she'd still run into some technical problems applying for school, but this was what she wanted to do.

Cam was recuperating, though she was still a little afraid she'd hug him too hard and he'd keel over. It was difficult to watch a strong man struggle with having some physical limitations, but there was such a wonderful feeling in helping him sometimes. In that process of helping him, she'd received the best gift of all from Cam.

She knew what she wanted to do with her life. The college applications were to local nursing programs. If that didn't work out, Hilly would find something else similar, something in the medical field to help people. One way or another.

Satisfied, she placed the applications on the kitchen table. She'd spent the first week after everything had gone down in Sarah's house in Cheyenne, but she hadn't liked it. Too many buildings, too many people.

Zach had laughed at her when she'd told him that, because in the grand scheme of things, Cheyenne was on the small side. Still, Hilly had wanted to go back to Bent. It truly was small and she could go out to her mountains that felt like home whenever she wanted.

She knew it hurt Sarah some, but Hilly had promised herself to spend this first year of freedom doing what felt right, what she wanted. At the end of the year, she'd reevaluate.

She visited James in jail weekly, and she was prepared to testify on his behalf when his case went to court. Zach hadn't been pleased, but he'd listened to her. Sarah had supported her wholeheartedly, though Hilly knew some of that stemmed from being desperate to forge a positive relationship with the daughter she'd thought she'd lost.

Hilly had gone with Zach once to visit Ethan in the care center he'd been assigned to. It had been difficult for all of them, but he did seem to be making some progress.

It was a weird thing, this life in the outside world. Thrilling and challenging. Wonderful and painful. In the end, she was so, so glad to be exactly here. Living both sides of it.

A knock sounded on the door, then it opened. Cam stepped in.

Hilly fixed him with a stern look. "You better have the doctor's permission to be walking around without your cane, mister."

He grinned at her, and her stomach flopped pleasantly. Oh, she loved this man—a little more every day.

"Just came from my checkup. Cleared to

walk without a cane. Assured I shouldn't have to have any more surgeries."

She crossed to him and gave him a gentle hug. "That's great news."

He nodded toward the table full of applications. "What's all this?"

She'd kept the college plans a secret from everyone except Sarah. It had been strangely nice to have a secret with her mother. She was getting closer and closer to thinking of Sarah as her mother.

"I'm going to try to go to nursing school," she said, pressing a hand to her stomach. Planning her life in the outside world still caught her sideways sometimes. Scary and thrilling and with a whirlwind of choices that left her breathless. Even though she was sure, it was still a whole *thing*.

"Hil. That's great. That's *perfect*." He squeezed her tight. "You'll be a fantastic nurse."

She squeezed him back. Her Cam. Always ready to hold her hand and be her anchor. To support her and encourage her.

They'd had their first date, and a few more since he'd been out of the hospital. Tonight she'd be by his side at Laurel and Grady's wedding. It was wonderful. The *them* they were building.

Of course, there was more she wanted, but

she'd held off because of his injuries. He'd hate if he knew that was why, so she hadn't told him.

But he was walking without his cane, and his color was back. She knew he was still in pain sometimes, but he was healing. They were both healing.

"I know we were supposed to go out to lunch before we got ready for the wedding, but—"

"You want to work on your applications. That's fine. I can—"

"No. That isn't what I want to do," she said, taking his hand. She led him to the bedroom.

He was grinning when she turned to him inside the room. She wrapped her arms around his neck and he pulled her close.

"I love you, Hilly," he said seriously. So serious. So sure. So *good*. And so very hers.

"I love you, too." Without a doubt. She might still be ignorant about a lot of things in the outside world, but the one thing she'd been given her whole life, even from a complicated man who'd done some bad things, was love. And now she'd been opened up to so much more.

So, she'd believe in it. Always.

\* \* \* \* \*

# Get 4 FREE REWARDS!

### We'll send you 2 FREE Books plus 2 FREE Mystery Gifts.

**Harlequin® Romantic Suspense** books feature heart-racing sensuality and the promise of a sweeping romance set against the backdrop of suspense.

**FREE**
Value Over
**$20**

---

**YES!** Please send me 2 FREE Harlequin® Romantic Suspense novels and my 2 FREE gifts (gifts are worth about $10 retail). After receiving them, if I don't wish to receive any more books, I can return the shipping statement marked "cancel." If I don't cancel, I will receive 4 brand-new novels every month and be billed just $4.99 per book in the U.S. or $5.74 per book in Canada. That's a savings of at least 12% off the cover price! It's quite a bargain! Shipping and handling is just 50¢ per book in the U.S. and 75¢ per book in Canada.* I understand that accepting the 2 free books and gifts places me under no obligation to buy anything. I can always return a shipment and cancel at any time. The free books and gifts are mine to keep no matter what I decide.

240/340 HDN GMYZ

Name (please print)

Address                                                                 Apt. #

City                             State/Province                    Zip/Postal Code

> Mail to the **Reader Service:**
> **IN U.S.A.:** P.O. Box 1341, Buffalo, NY 14240-8531
> **IN CANADA:** P.O. Box 603, Fort Erie, Ontario L2A 5X3

**Want to try 2 free books from another series!** Call 1-800-873-8635 or visit www.ReaderService.com.

---

# Get 4 FREE REWARDS!

## We'll send you 2 FREE Books
## <u>plus</u> 2 FREE Mystery Gifts.

**Harlequin Presents®** books feature a sensational and sophisticated world of international romance where sinfully tempting heroes ignite passion.

FREE
Value Over
**$20**

---

# READERSERVICE.COM

## Manage your account online!

- Review your order history
- Manage your payments
- Update your address

*We've designed the
Reader Service website
just for you.*

## Enjoy all the features!

- Discover new series available to you, and read excerpts from any series.
- Respond to mailings and special monthly offers.
- Browse the Bonus Bucks catalog and online-only exculsives.
- Share your feedback.

*Visit us at:*

## ReaderService.com